# Anna Mei, Cartoon Girl

# Anna Mei
## Cartoon Girl

By Carol A. Grund

Pauline
BOOKS & MEDIA
Boston

Library of Congress Cataloging-in-Publication Data
Grund, Carol A.
 Anna Mei, cartoon girl / by Carol A. Grund.
  p. cm.
 Summary: When eleven-year-old Anna Mei, who was adopted from China, moves from Boston to small-town Michigan, she finds herself questioning her identity, family history, and more as she seeks a way to fit in.
 ISBN 0-8198-0788-5 (pbk.)
 [1. Moving, Household--Fiction. 2. Adoption--Fiction. 3. Chinese Americans--Fiction. 4. Schools--Fiction. 5. Identity--Fiction. 6. Individuality--Fiction. 7. Family life--Michigan--Fiction. 8. Michigan--Fiction.] I. Title.
 PZ7.G9328Ann 2010
 [Fic]--dc22

                    2009031628

Many manufacturers and sellers distinguish their products through the use of trademarks. Any trademarked designations that appear in this book are used in good faith but are not authorized by, associated with, or sponsored by the trademark owners.

Cover art by Wayne Alfano
Back cover calligraphy by Eping Wei
Design by Mary Joseph Peterson, FSP

"P" and PAULINE are registered trademarks of the Daughters of St. Paul.

Published by Pauline Books & Media, 50 Saint Pauls Avenue, Boston, MA 02130-3491

Printed in the U.S.A.

AMI VSAUSAPEOILL03-1009-09458 0788-5

www.pauline.org

Pauline Books & Media is the publishing house of the Daughters of St. Paul, an international congregation of women religious serving the Church with the communications media.

1 2 3 4 5 6 7 8 9                                  13 12 11 10

For Jim, who is my heart;
Matthew, Paul, and David,
who are my light and inspiration;
my parents, who provided merely
a lifetime of support;
and my editor extraordinaire,
Diane, who coaxed Anna Mei
out of the desk drawer
and gave her a home.

# Contents

# Chapter One

# The New Kid

Anna Mei squeezed between the packing boxes scattered around her bedroom, trying to see into the mirror propped against a wall.

She knew her jeans were okay. They were new without being I-got-these-at-the-mall-yesterday new. And she couldn't go wrong with layered T-shirts, purple over white. It was the shoes she needed to check out—the hot-pink sneakers with silver laces, the ones she had chosen months ago at the department store back home in Boston.

They'd seemed so cute then, so perfect for starting sixth grade. But now that they were on her feet, and her feet were far from home, she worried they might be perfect only if your goal was getting laughed back into *fifth* grade.

"Anna Mei!" her mother called from downstairs. "You don't want to be late on your very first day!"

"Guess again," she answered, too softly for her mother to hear. But Cleo heard, and she came to sympathize by rubbing against Anna Mei's leg.

"I wish I could stay here with you," Anna Mei told her, reaching down to stroke the cat's gray and white fur. "But Mom and Dad have this crazy idea that I should go to school today."

In fact, her parents had been full of crazy ideas lately. It had really started a year ago, when Anna Mei's grandmother died. She and Anna Mei's mother had been very close, so it was no surprise that Mom took it pretty hard. The surprise came on the day her parents announced they were moving to Michigan. Mom decided she wanted to be near the only family she had left, and that meant the small town where her sister—Anna Mei's Aunt Karen—lived with her husband and two kids.

Of course Anna Mei had tried to talk them out of it, but their minds were made up. Her father had already taken a job doing research for a university, and her mother planned to find a nursing job as soon as they were settled. All through the weeks of packing, they kept insisting that their new life in Michigan would be as good as the old one in Massachusetts. *Better*, in fact. Even when unexpected delays meant Anna Mei would miss the first two weeks of school, they had assured her that everything would be all right. No worries. Greener pastures awaited. Happy days were—

"Anna Mei!"

Mom's voice had reached final warning mode.

"Coming!" Anna Mei called. With a last despairing glance at the possibly dopey shoes, she grabbed her backpack and headed downstairs.

Although she would normally take the bus to Elmwood Elementary, her mother had insisted on driving her today. So Anna Mei wasn't surprised that they were barely out of the driveway when the pep talk started.

"Don't worry, honey," Mom said, turning out of their neighborhood and onto a main road. "It will be hard at first, missing your friends back in Boston. I miss mine, too."

Anna Mei turned her face toward the window. Surely her mother didn't expect *sympathy,* not when this had all been her idea in the first place.

"I still think it's the right thing to do, in the long run," Mom continued. "In the short run, well . . . I'm just trying to tell you that it will get easier as time goes on. I promise."

Today, more than any other so far, Anna Mei didn't trust herself to talk about it. If she fell apart now, she'd never manage to get through the next few minutes, let alone the whole day. Her only hope was to push away all thoughts of her home and school and the friends she'd known since kindergarten.

That strategy lasted approximately three minutes. The moment they pulled into the school parking lot alongside all the cars and buses filled with strangers, Anna Mei felt a wave of panic rise up. She closed her eyes and summoned up a prayer from somewhere deep inside. *Dear God, please help me get through this day. I don't think I can do it alone.*

A few kids stopped to stare as she and her mother walked into the school office, but when a bell rang they scurried off like ants late for a picnic.

An older woman looked up from her desk. "May I help you?"

"Hello, I'm Margaret Anderson," Mom said. "This is my daughter's first day here."

"Welcome to Elmwood," the woman said. "I'm Mrs. Marshall, the school secretary. We've been expecting you, Anna Mei. Is that right? *May,* like the month?"

Anna Mei nodded, wishing for about the billionth time that her parents had named her something normal, like Jessica or Ashley.

"That's very pretty," Mrs. Marshall said. Probably *Jessica* Marshall.

The secretary picked up a file folder and looked inside. "I have some forms to go over with your mother," she said to Anna Mei, "but since the bell has already rung, I'll take you to your classroom first."

She consulted the file again. "You've been assigned to Ms. Wagner's homeroom. You'll be her twenty-fourth student." Anna Mei's face must have shown some of the panic she was trying to hide, because Mrs. Marshall's voice suddenly softened. "I'm sure you'll make lots of friends in no time."

Anna Mei choked back a bitter reply. After all, she'd seen enough new kids over the years to know how it really worked. They were the ones you saw standing around, shuffling their feet, looking at the floor and wondering where they were going to sit. She had just never imagined that one day she'd be one of them.

Leaving her mother at the office, she followed Mrs. Marshall through a maze of hallways, feeling more and more lost. Honestly, if this whole Elmwood thing didn't work out, she'd never be able to find her way out of here.

Mrs. Marshall finally stopped in front of a door marked 117. She tapped on it softly and pushed it open. "Excuse me, Ms. Wagner," she said, "your new student is here."

A voice from inside the room answered, "Thank you. Please send her in."

Mrs. Marshall gave Anna Mei's shoulder a quick squeeze. "You'll be just fine," she whispered, then turned away and disappeared back down the hall. Anna Mei had to fight the urge to follow her. After all, a school secretary could always use some extra help around the office, couldn't she?

Instead she took a deep breath and stepped into the room, where twenty-three pairs of eyes were all focused on just one thing—the new kid.

# Chapter Two

# *Lucky* Student Number 24

Ms. Wagner stood at her desk, holding what looked like an attendance book.

"Attention, sixth graders," she said, as if every sixth grader within miles had not already frozen in place. "This is our new student, Anna Mei Anderson, who has just moved here from Boston. Come right in, Anna Mei."

Anna Mei closed the door behind her and took a few steps into the room, guided by the warm smile Ms. Wagner was beaming her way. She seemed on the youngish side as far as teachers go, with blue eyes behind dark-framed glasses and light brown hair that just touched her shoulders.

"We're very happy to have you join us," Ms. Wagner said. "I know everyone will do his or her best to make you feel welcome."

"Thank you," Anna Mei managed to say, forcing the words through dry lips.

"I'm looking forward to—yes, Danny, what is it? Do you have a question?"

A boy with rust-colored hair and a sprinkling of freckles had raised his hand. "I just want to know why she's named after a cartoon," he said.

Ms. Wagner frowned. "I don't understand what you mean."

"Anna Mei," he said, as if that explained everything. When Ms. Wagner still looked puzzled, he tried again. "It's a kind of cartoon. You know, like Pokémon or Dragon Ball Z."

A girl sitting near the window groaned. "Danny Gallagher, that is *so* dumb."

But Ms. Wagner was nodding. "Actually, I see what he's getting at," she said. Stepping over to the whiteboard, she picked up a blue marker and wrote:

## anime

"This is the word for a style of animation that originated in Japan. I'm sure most of you have heard of it—it's become quite popular here in the United States. And it *is* pronounced *anna-may*. So Danny is not too far off." A trace of a smile flashed across her face. "*This* time."

Another hand shot up. Anna Mei felt as though she'd accidentally stumbled onto a game show, where they stuck you under a spotlight and forced you to answer a bunch of questions. Only instead of a million dollars, or even a year's supply of frozen dinners, she was playing for the chance to be Lucky Student Number 24.

"So, are you Japanese?" asked a girl with a long blond ponytail and bright orange shirt.

Anna Mei swallowed hard. Would that lump sitting in her throat *ever* go away?

"No," she said, relieved that her voice had worked its way around the lump. "I was born in China. But I left there when I was a baby, so I don't remember it. I've always lived in Boston."

"You mean, like, next to the ocean?" another girl wanted to know.

"Well, *Boston* is next to the ocean, but it's a really big city. Our house was in a suburb about a half hour away from the water." For just a moment an uninvited image of the home she'd left behind pushed itself into her mind. She took a breath and forced herself to go on. "But we went into the city a lot, for shopping and museums and shows."

Ms. Wagner had a question of her own. "Do you have any brothers and sisters?" she asked.

"No, just my parents," Anna Mei said. "But now we live near my cousins and my aunt."

"Your *what*?" asked a boy in the front row. "Did you say *ahhh-nt*?"

His exaggerated pronunciation made the rest of the kids laugh. Anna Mei felt her cheeks flush hot.

Suddenly the game show had turned into a sitcom, with her as the punch line.

"Class!" Ms. Wagner said sharply, her smile disappearing. "I will not tolerate rudeness. The fact is that the same word is often pronounced differently in different parts of the country."

She turned to the whiteboard again. Under the word *anime* she wrote

## aunt

The way things were going, Anna Mei expected *awful* would be next.

"Here in the Midwest we say *ant*," Ms. Wagner explained, "but Anna Mei is from the Northeast, where they pronounce it *ah-nt*. Both are correct."

She set her marker on the ledge. "I think we've had enough questions for today. Anna Mei, I'm looking forward to getting to know you. You'll start here each morning for a short homeroom session, followed by social studies. Then the whole class moves to other rooms and other teachers through the fifth- and sixth-grade wing. At the end of the day you'll come back here for science, followed by announcements and dismissal."

Ms. Wagner walked back to her desk, her eyes sweeping the room to be sure she had everyone's attention. "I know that every student here will be happy to answer any questions you have as you learn your way around. Please go ahead and choose an empty seat, and we'll continue with announcements."

Anna Mei scooted quickly to the back of the room and slid into a desk, grateful that Ms. Wagner didn't have one of those charts where all the kids whose last names started with "A" had to sit in front.

"All right, class," Ms. Wagner said, "my last announcement has to do with some of the special projects I'm planning for the next few months. I think you'll find them pretty exciting."

Although no one groaned out loud, Anna Mei could practically hear eye-rolling going on all over the classroom. After all, sixth graders have learned enough to be skeptical whenever a teacher calls an assignment "exciting."

A boy sitting near the front raised his hand.

"Yes, Luis?"

"You mean, like field trips?" he asked. "Last year we got to go to the planetarium and Spartan Stadium. Some of the football players gave us a tour."

"Well, yes, we'll probably plan a few trips," Ms. Wagner said, "but right now I'm talking about projects. For example, in science you'll be building some unique terrariums. And for social studies, you'll be working on heritage projects."

The room was silent for a moment, and then the red-haired boy sitting next to Anna Mei spoke up. "Are you sure we can't just go to Spartan Stadium again?" he asked.

*Danny,* she remembered. He was the one who had started the whole cartoon discussion. *Thanks a lot, Danny.*

"I'm sure of only one thing," Ms. Wagner told him, "and that is that you are going to stop blurting out remarks without being called on. Understood?"

"I'll try, Ms. Wagner," he said. He caught Anna Mei looking at him and flashed a smile. She turned away quickly. He had a lot of nerve—first picking on her and then trying to act all friendly. She may not know much about Elmwood Elementary yet, but she could certainly figure out which kids to stay away from. And Danny Gallagher already owned the top spot on *that* list.

# Chapter Three

# Today's Special

Anna Mei glared at the clock, as if sheer will-power could make the hands move faster. Somehow she seemed to have entered an alternate universe, where time had slowed to the pace of a giant tortoise, out for a stroll in the sun.

She'd been in class with two other teachers since leaving Ms. Wagner's room, and both had seemed nice enough. But she just couldn't seem to concentrate on things like decimals and dangling modifiers. She couldn't stop thinking about her old school, and the places where she thought she'd be spending this day. If she'd known she wouldn't be going back there, she would have appreciated it more, even the boring parts. She'd have realized what it meant to be in a place that felt safe and familiar, where you had memorized every crack in every tile in every hallway, and where people smiled at you instead of staring.

When the bell finally rang for lunch, Anna Mei realized she had a new problem—figuring out how to get from Point A (this classroom, located somewhere deep inside Elmwood Elementary School) to Point B (the cafeteria, location unknown). The room was emptying pretty quickly, so she decided to play follow-the-leader, fixing her eyes on the girl with the blond ponytail who'd been sitting in front of her.

She followed the girl into the hallway and was immediately swept up into a river of kids flowing toward the cafeteria, one hallway over. Once there, everyone split into groups, some joining the hot-lunch line and others going straight to the long tables to eat lunches they'd brought from home. When the girl sat down at a table near the door, Anna Mei slipped in beside her, hoping no one would notice.

All the kids seemed to be talking at once, as if their voices had been locked up all morning and had just burst free. The chatter swirled around her, mixing with what was apparently a universal school-cafeteria smell—a mixture of not-quite-sour-yet milk and today's special, which her nose identified as either lasagna or spaghetti.

Among the sounds and smells, Anna Mei began to relax a little. She felt almost invisible as she pulled a sandwich and fruit cup from her lunch bag and began to eat. So it took a few minutes before she noticed that the conversation had died down, and that several of the girls at her table were staring at her.

"What?" she asked, grabbing her napkin, figuring she must have a mustard blob on her chin, or something equally mortifying.

"Nothing," one of them said. "It's just that, well, some people thought you might eat your lunch with chopsticks."

A girl sitting across the table from her sighed heavily.

"Maybe some *immature* people thought that," she said, in a tone that made it clear she was certainly not one of them. "I mean, just because she's *Chinese* doesn't mean she's going to run around in a kimono eating fortune cookies, right?"

Anna Mei thought the question might be directed at her, but if it was, the girl didn't wait for an answer. "I'm Zoey," she said instead, then pointed to the others. "This is Rachel, and this is Amber."

"Hi," Anna Mei said to all of them in general, managing a smile.

Amber, the blond girl Anna Mei had followed, grinned broadly, showing two rows of bright green braces. Up close, her orange shirt was patterned all over with tiny pink hearts. "We all think it's *so* cool that you lived in Boston," she told Anna Mei. "I love big cities. Boston's not as big as New York, though. My family went to New York once, at Christmastime. We saw the Rockettes and everything."

"I can't wait to go there!" chimed in the girl sitting across from Amber—Rachel. Her hair was almost as dark as Anna Mei's but much curlier, with some of the curls escaping from her ponytail and making a frame around her face. Her eyebrows made perfect arches above her dark eyes. A black and white shirt paired with black jeans and short boots made her look like she'd stepped out of a magazine ad.

"My mom promised to take me when I'm sixteen," Rachel said. "She says New York has the best shopping in the world. This whole town would practically fit into one of their department stores."

This brought another deep sigh from Zoey, who had finished her sandwich and was slowly peeling an orange. Although all three girls were taller than Anna Mei, Zoey was definitely the tallest, and her light-brown ponytail hung almost all the way down her back. She had wide blue-green eyes, probably made bluer by the soft shade of her denim jacket.

"I guess New York and Boston are okay," she said, making *okay* sound like *not really worth my time*. "Personally I'd rather go to Kentucky. That's where all the best tracks and farms are."

"That's true," Rachel agreed. "Maybe my mom will take me there, too. I'd love to visit Churchill Downs in person."

"How about you, Anna Mei?" Amber asked. "Do you ride?"

Now they were all looking at her again, waiting for an answer. Anna Mei struggled to connect the dots of this weird conversation. Rockettes, Churchill Downs, ride . . . ?

Sudden inspiration hit her. "You mean . . . horses?" she asked.

"Well, *yeah*," Zoey said as the other two giggled. "Of course horses. Isn't that what we're talking about?"

*Don't ask me!* Anna Mei thought, but aloud she said, "I've been to a riding stable a couple of times. I don't know if—"

She never had a chance to finish that thought, because right in the middle of it, a voice rang out loud enough for the whole cafeteria to hear.

# Chapter Four

# The Ponytail Club

"Hey!" said the voice. "It's Cartoon Girl!"

Balancing a lunch tray in one hand and a milk carton in the other, Danny Gallagher had stopped at their table on his way to the trash can.

Rachel frowned. "Not funny, Danny."

"Yeah, Danny, get lost," Amber said.

"For your *information*," Zoey announced, her words practically dripping with disgust, "her name is *Anna Mei.*"

Danny took a noisy slurp of milk. "That's what I *said*—Cartoon Girl!" Then he flashed a grin and was gone.

"Ugh," Zoey said, summing up Anna Mei's feelings exactly. "Don't let him get to you. He's always making stupid jokes like that. He thinks he's funny."

Rachel wadded up her empty paper bag. "Yeah, just ignore him," she advised. "That's what we do. That's what *everyone* does."

Anna Mei thought that might be harder than they made it sound, especially if Danny continued to pop up out of nowhere just to make fun of her.

"Anyway." And with that one word Zoey took back control of the conversation. "We have this horse club, called the Ponytails. Get it?" She pulled her own long ponytail over one shoulder, running her hand through it like a comb. "We're having a meeting at Rachel's on Friday after school. You should come."

For the first time all day Anna Mei felt a glimmer of hope. Maybe she wouldn't end up being the loneliest kid at Elmwood Elementary after all.

"So, do you all have horses?" she asked.

Rachel sighed. "I wish."

"Don't we all," Amber agreed.

"*Well*," Zoey said, "none of us actually *has* one. But we're going to someday."

"For now we just talk about them," Amber said. "And read magazines, trade books, watch horse movies, stuff like that. It's fun."

"I'll ask my parents," Anna Mei said, then quickly added, "thanks."

She hadn't found horses to be all that fascinating before, but you never knew—maybe she'd been missing something. And besides, any kind of club was better than none, no matter what it was about. Any new kid knew that.

As it turned out, her parents not only said she could go to Rachel's house, they practically turned cartwheels when they heard that Anna Mei had been invited somewhere already.

The three of them—four if you counted Cleo, slinking around under the table and stalking stray food crumbs—had gathered to eat their first home-cooked meal in the new house. Until then they'd been eating microwave and take-out stuff. Most of the pots and pans were still in boxes marked KITCHEN. But today her mother had shopped for groceries and organized the cupboards, at least enough to put together some beef stew, fresh bread, and green beans.

Anna Mei closed her eyes as she joined in the prayer of thanks they always said before meals. It seemed strange to be saying the familiar words in this unfamiliar place. It made her feel less homesick and more homesick, both at the same time.

Then Mom lifted her water glass. "To your first day of sixth grade," she said, and they all clinked their glasses together.

"Sounds like you're off to a good start," Dad said, "making friends on your very first day." He took a piece of bread and passed the basket to Anna Mei.

"Those girls you told me about sound very nice," Mom said, smiling. "Zoey and Rachel and . . . Amy?"

Anna Mei sighed. Now they'd be expecting her to go floating off to school every day on fluffy pink clouds or something. Time for a reality check.

"It's Amber," she said. "And they're okay, I guess. But it felt like everyone was staring at me all the time. Maybe they think it's weird that I'm Chinese. No one at my old school ever cared about that."

"That's because they grew up with you," Mom said, spreading butter on her bread. "I'm sure these kids are just curious."

"Margaret, this stew is fantastic," Dad said. "I don't think my stomach could have managed one more pizza." He took another bite, then said to Anna Mei, "Remember, this is a much smaller town than what we're used to. Of course there aren't as many Asian kids at the school. Pretty soon no one will even notice, you'll see."

"What about your teachers?" Mom asked. "What were they like?"

Anna Mei shrugged. "Okay so far. My homeroom teacher is Ms. Wagner. Then I had Mr. Vogel for English and Mrs. Stanton for math. She was teaching stuff about decimals that I already learned last year. I also had gym. Did you know they call sneakers *tennis shoes* here? Weird."

Dad took a second helping of stew. "That's all

well and good," he said, "but I'm still waiting to hear about the *really* important class."

"Hmmmm, I wonder what *that* could be," Anna Mei said, but she couldn't help smiling.

Never mind that she was adopted, her father always said, she'd managed to inherit his love for science anyway. She'd spent her childhood peering up at the stars, poking around in the dirt, trying to discover what made the world tick. She never got grossed out in school when they had to examine slugs or study the digestive system. "I *love* this stuff," she'd say enthusiastically, as kids all around her threatened to barf.

"Ms. Wagner did say something about terrariums," she said. "I think we're going to build some and then observe what happens in them."

"Ah, the scientific method," Dad said, using his nerdy professor voice. "Excellent. Let me know if you need any help with that."

"Meanwhile, *I* could use some help," Mom announced, "particularly with these dishes."

"Sorry, I'm only interested in petrie dishes," Dad answered, winking at Anna Mei. She groaned out loud. Not only was her father a self-proclaimed science geek, he was the king of bad jokes.

"I'll help, Mom," Anna Mei said, "I don't have much homework tonight. But I'm going to need the computer pretty soon. When do you think we'll have Internet hookup?"

"I'll call tomorrow and schedule it," her mother promised.

"Well, since I can't go online yet, would it be okay if I called Lauren? I want to tell her about school and stuff."

Lauren had been her best friend since the first grade. When Anna Mei told her she was moving, Lauren had cried as though her heart would break. And even though it happened months ago, the memory of that day still made Anna Mei's throat ache.

"Sure," Mom answered. "Just let me know when you're finished so I can call Aunt Karen. We're making plans to get together soon."

Now that they lived less than an hour from Aunt Karen, the two families would be spending a lot more time together. Anna Mei had always enjoyed the occasional visits with her aunt and uncle. And her cousins were fun to play with. Six-year-old Emily loved board games and was learning to read. Benjamin, almost a year old, could sit up alone now and had started to crawl.

Still, Anna Mei would much rather be calling them on the phone and getting together with Lauren, instead of the other way around.

# Chapter Five

# Ugly Bedroom Blues

"Cleo! This is *not* helping!"

Every time Anna Mei opened one of the boxes scattered around the room, the cat meowed with pleasure and jumped in to investigate. Anna Mei had already dragged her out of a stack of sweaters and rescued a stuffed hippo Cleo had batted under the bed. It sure wasn't making the job go any faster.

Not that she had anything better to do, sadly. Saturday afternoon used to mean hanging out with Lauren, going swimming or bowling or just sitting around in each other's bedrooms, talking. But this Saturday afternoon stretched out endlessly, with no place to go and no one to talk to. She'd thought that unpacking would be better than nothing, but now she wasn't so sure.

"Mom!" she called down the stairs. "Do we have any more hangers?"

"Just a minute, I'll see what I can find," her mother called back.

While she waited, Anna Mei sat on the floor and started poking through a box labeled A-M BOOKS. In her old bedroom, she'd had a built-in bookcase with lots of shelves. Where was she supposed to put her books in here? It was an ugly room anyway, with ratty beige carpet and dark green curtains. Worst of all was the wallpaper, a nightmare of leafy ivy plants creeping up white trellises. Ugh.

Her mother appeared in the doorway with a handful of hangers. "Need some help in here?"

"Don't I have any horse books?" Anna Mei asked her. "Rachel has a whole bookshelf full, and I can't even find one."

"Well, you were never very interested in horse books before," Mom reminded her. "Is that what you did at your meeting yesterday? Read books?"

"No, but all the girls brought some to trade," she said. "Mostly they just talked about riding. And Rachel had a DVD called *Dreamer*. We watched that for a while, even though Zoey said they'd seen it about a hundred times already. I guess they wanted me to see it."

Her mother knelt down and started pulling books out of the box. "I'm glad you had fun," she said.

"Well, I wouldn't exactly . . ." Anna Mei started to say. Then she hesitated. It was probably easier just to let her mother believe that, at least for now. The truth was that she had felt pretty weird the whole time. While Zoey, Amber, and Rachel had chatted about bloodlines and currycombs and English saddles versus Western, Anna Mei had smiled lamely, pretending to be interested. Uncomfortable, for sure. But fun? Not even close.

"Aha!" Mom said, pulling a copy of *The Black Stallion* from the box. "And there are a couple of Misty books, too. Will those work?"

"They're pretty old," Anna Mei decided. "I'm sure the other girls have already read them. Could we go to the bookstore and get some new ones?"

Her mother stood up, brushing off the knees of her jeans. She was tall, even in stocking feet. Anna Mei's father always said she could have been a model if the nursing thing hadn't worked out. He joked that her patients probably thought they'd died and gone to heaven when they saw this blond, blue-eyed angel hovering over them.

"I can't take you today," she said. "I'm working on my résumé so I can start job hunting. But we'll go before your next meeting, okay?"

"Okay, thanks."

"And . . . sweetie? You know it's not the books that are important, right? Those girls will like you just for yourself, as soon as they get to know you."

Anna Mei sank down on the bed, pulling Cleo into her lap so her hands would have something to do. She knew her mother believed that, but what if it wasn't true? What if they got to know her and didn't like her at all? Then she wouldn't be just the new girl or the Chinese girl—she'd be the girl without any friends.

"I hope so," she said finally, not feeling ready to put those fears into words yet.

Her mother started picking up sweaters and putting them on hangers. "This is a nice big closet," she said. "It looks like everything will fit, with room left over."

"I guess so . . . but Mom? This wallpaper? It's really gross."

"What are you saying? That you're not into the whole garden terrace look?"

Anna Mei snorted. "Maybe if I was, like, fifty or something."

Mom laughed. "Okay, I get it. If this were one of those decorating shows, your room would definitely be the *before*. What did you have in mind?"

Anna Mei didn't hesitate. "I want it to be like my old room," she said, "with a bookshelf here, and my desk over there, and the walls painted—"

"—pink!" they finished at the same time.

"Well, it *is* my favorite color," Anna Mei said, feeling a little resentful that she had to defend it. After all, did *everything* have to change?

"I just thought you might want something different this time, that's all," Mom said. "I'll tell you what—let's pick up a few paint chips when we're out shopping. Then we'll sort of casually leave them around, to ease your dad into the whole idea."

Anna Mei knew the routine. Home improvement projects had to be handled diplomatically with her father, who was practically allergic to them. He always said he was more at home with a test tube than a paintbrush. But even he would have to admit that this was one ugly room.

Her mother had finished with the sweaters. "Looks like you've got most of the boxes emptied," she said. "I need to get back to my résumé, so keep up the good—"

She stopped in midsentence, her gaze fixed on the dresser where Anna Mei had placed some framed photos. One was of her with Lauren on their First Communion day, dressed in floaty white dresses and standing together in front of St. Cecelia's back home. But it was the other frame that Anna Mei's mother picked up, the one with the photo someone had taken in Yiyang on the first day the Andersons had arrived there. A tall, blue-eyed blond couple stood on the steps of the orphanage, their faces radiant, their arms cradling a tiny, dark-haired baby girl.

"How is it possible that you're almost twelve years old already?" Mom asked, her voice sounding a little shaky as she touched her finger to the glass. "I'll never forget that day. I was so happy to have you for my very own daughter."

"Oh, Mom," Anna Mei said, surprised when her own voice came out shaky, too.

"Daughter of my heart," her mother said, bending down to kiss the top of Anna Mei's head. It was a phrase she had repeated often over the years, but this time, for some reason, the familiar words made Anna Mei's eyes prickle with tears.

# Chapter Six

# Science Partners

That's all I can think of to tell you for now. If anything interesting ever happens here I'll let you know. Tell everyone there I said hi and write back soon!!!

Anna Mei's father had found her at the kitchen table, typing on the laptop. "Is that homework?" he asked, looking at his watch and frowning. "I hope it's not due today."

"No," she said. "I'm e-mailing Lauren."

"Well, wrap it up," he told her. "Your mom had to leave early for her interview, but I can drive you to school if we leave now. I have to be at a meeting in an hour."

"Okay, I'll be right there. I have to grab something out of the fridge first."

She ended her e-mail by typing "Your BFF," then hit SEND. With any luck, Lauren would see it and write back today. Although, judging from all her talk lately about swimming practice and choir rehearsal, Lauren might be too busy to answer anytime soon.

Anna Mei had been in Michigan for a month now, and every day she felt her old life slipping farther away. Lauren and her other friends were probably used to her being gone by now. After all, their lives hadn't really changed much. She was the one living in no-man's-land—not part of the old life anymore but not really part of this one, either.

The days seemed to crawl by, and today seemed even longer than usual because it was Friday. Finally it was time for science, the last class of the day. Ms. Wagner began with an announcement.

"We're starting our terrarium projects today," she said. "I have twelve large plastic jars, so you'll be working in pairs. Did everyone bring in their assignments from yesterday?"

The assignment had been one of the weirdest Anna Mei ever had. Ms. Wagner told them to bring in their leftover food from dinner—bread, salad, fruit, vegetables—pretty much anything except meat.

"Most people think of a terrarium as a place where plants grow, or maybe a place to keep a lizard," Ms. Wagner was saying. "But yours are going to be a little unusual. Yours are going to be mold terrariums."

"What kind?" Zandra asked, her eyes widening.

"You're kidding!" Luis said. Then he grinned. "Cool."

"It *is* cool," Ms. Wagner agreed. "Just wait until you see what these jars look like in a few weeks."

Zoey made a face that said she could pretty much imagine what they'd look like—and smell like, too. "Disgusting, that's what," she said, and some of the other girls jumped in to agree.

"Maybe," Ms. Wagner said, "but still pretty cool. You'll start by making a hypothesis. As you know, that just means writing down your guess about what you think will happen to your food samples. Over the next few weeks you'll record your observations. Finally, you'll describe your results and determine if your hypothesis was correct."

Anna Mei had to smile. *There you go, Dad,* she thought. *The scientific method rules!*

But her amusement changed to horror when Ms. Wagner, walking along the rows and distributing the jars, handed one to her and said, "Anna Mei, you'll be working with Danny for this project. Here's a plastic knife, a paper cup for water—don't spill it, Danny— and a list of instructions. It's very important that you follow them exactly."

Then she moved on to the next row, completely unaware of the devastation she'd left behind.

Danny seemed unaware of it, too. "Okay, partner," he said to Anna Mei, "let's see what you had for dinner last night."

She frowned. *Not Chinese food, if that's what you're thinking.* "I brought a piece of baked potato, a cooked carrot, and a muffin," she said.

"And I've got some shredded cheese, lettuce, and a piece of taco shell." He unwrapped a paper napkin with Taco City written on it. "My dad had to work late so my brother got us some take-out. I also brought half a banana from breakfast and—hold on . . ."

He pulled something out of his jeans pocket. "My cookie from lunch. I was saving it for later but I guess I can donate it to the cause."

*Great*, Anna Mei thought, trying not to look at the brown, crumbled mess. *Thanks.*

Danny grabbed for the jar but she yanked it out of his reach. "If you don't *mind*," she said, "I'd like to read the instructions first."

He shrugged. "Go for it. I personally already know how to open a jar."

Another day, another lame Danny joke. Anna Mei ignored it and began reading the instructions out loud. "Use the knife to cut food samples into small pieces. You will need only a few pieces of each kind."

"Got it," Danny said, sawing away enthusiastically at the food scraps. "Then what?"

"Dip each piece in the water, then put them carefully in the jar. Try to spread them out so they're not touching each other."

All around the room, Anna Mei heard other kids joking and giggling as they prepared their own terrariums, sounding as if they were enjoying the unusual assignment. Of course, none of *them* had gotten stuck with the biggest jerk in the whole class for a partner.

The final step was to seal the lid shut with tape and initial it so they could tell the jars apart. "After labeling your jar," Anna Mei read, "check the food for changes each day, recording your observations in a notebook."

"You should be the one who records stuff," Danny said. "I'm more of an artist type."

This didn't exactly qualify as news to Anna Mei. Sitting at the desk right across from his, she couldn't help noticing the assortment of sketchbooks he doodled in on a regular basis.

Now he was using a felt-tip marker to draw a design on the jar lid. Finally he added some curlicue lettering.

"See?" he asked.

She saw, all right. The initials he'd written on their terrarium were "D.G." and "C.G."

# Chapter Seven

# *More* **Projects**

I t was the last straw. Not only did Danny plan to dump all the work on her, but he just wouldn't let that stupid Cartoon Girl thing go.

"Those are *not* my initials," Anna Mei told him through gritted teeth. "And if you want my help with this project, you'd better change them. *Now.*"

He shrugged. "If you say so," he said, as if she was the one with the problem. She watched as he transformed the "C.G." into some weird-looking squiggly creature, then squeezed "A.M.A." underneath it. Great. Now everyone would think that creature was a picture of *her.*

Anna Mei went to the sink to wash her hands, imagining Danny's head as she pounded hard on the soap dispenser. It just wasn't fair. She *loved* science class. Doing experiments and writing reports were pretty much the best things about school, as far as she was concerned. Now it was ruined, all because of Danny Gallagher.

Fifteen minutes later, the first observations had been recorded in everyone's notebooks, and the terrariums were lined up neatly on a shelf.

"All right, class," Ms. Wagner said, raising her hand to signal for their attention. "That's an excellent beginning to our experiment. You won't believe the changes you'll see when you observe the terrariums again on Monday. Now, since we have a few minutes before the bell rings, I'd like to talk about a couple of other projects you'll be working on soon."

Anna Mei slumped down in her seat, pretty sure she knew what was coming next.

"One will be your heritage project for social studies," Ms. Wagner said, and right on cue, Anna Mei's stomach did that little flip-flop thing it always did when this subject came up. After all, "heritage" meant ancestors, and how was she supposed to write about people she'd never even met?

"Of course, many of us have more than one kind of ethnic background," Ms. Wagner went on, apparently unwilling to let a little thing like Anna Mei's queasy stomach get in the way of her enthusiasm. "For example, I'm German on my father's side and French on my mother's. So for the purposes of this project, you may choose just one side of your heritage to talk about."

Anna Mei slumped down even lower. One side, two sides—what difference did it make to someone who had zero sides?

"The reports will be written, but you'll also be presenting them in front of the class. So I want you to include some kind of costume or visual aid that represents your family heritage. You might also want to bring a special food to share. For example, I could bring in some French croissants, or some German Wiener schnitzel."

If Ms. Wagner heard the soft giggles and snorts rippling through the room, she chose to ignore them. "I'll be handing out written instructions soon so you can get started," she said. "But there's something else that just came up, something that needs our immediate attention. It seems that the parent council has decided to organize a school carnival, and since you are the oldest students in the school, they'll be counting on you for help."

She explained that the carnival would be held in the school gym on the Friday before Halloween. Parent volunteers would organize games, raffles, and refreshments, while the sixth graders would be in charge of decorations. "We can use pumpkins, autumn leaves, scarecrows—whatever we can find or make inexpensively."

When the dismissal bell rang a few minutes later, it could barely be heard over the buzz of excitement in room 117. Everyone had ideas about what the carnival should be like.

"I can't wait!" Amber said, as she and Anna Mei headed into the hallway together. They caught up with Zoey and Rachel at the school entrance.

"I just hope it's not all for the little kids," Amber went on. "Wouldn't it be cool if there was a dunk tank, like the one at the county fair?"

"Great idea," Rachel agreed. "They could put the teachers in there. Then kids would line up for miles."

"Yeah, the parent council would make a fortune!" Amber said, laughing.

Of course Zoey had an idea superior to all the rest. "*I* know what would be cool. They should have a dance room, with a live DJ and strobe lights and—"

She stopped in midsentence, her gaze fixed on the parking lot where kids were loading noisily into cars and busses. "Is that lady waving at us?"

They all turned to look. Amid all the shouting and chaos, one woman stood alone by her car, looking directly at the girls and waving her arm. That woman was Mrs. Anderson.

"Um, you go ahead," Anna Mei said, feeling a redness start to creep up her neck and stain her face. "I'll catch up."

Before they could ask any questions, she scooted across the sidewalk and into the parking lot. Was her mother losing it or something? Had she forgotten today was Friday?

"Hi, honey!" Mom called out cheerfully. "Did you have a good day?"

"It was okay," Anna Mei said, "but what are you doing here? I'm supposed to go to Zoey's for a club meeting."

"I know, but I just couldn't wait to share my good news," Mom said, with a smile that made her whole face practically glow. "I went for my interview at the hospital this morning, and they hired me on the spot. They said I had just the experience they were looking for. Isn't that great?"

*Great* was not exactly the first word that jumped into Anna Mei's head. After all, her mother's new job would be just another link in the chain that kept her a prisoner here. But how could she say that when her mother seemed so happy about it? And besides, if they absolutely, positively *had* to live here, she was glad her mother would be doing the work she loved.

"That's really great, Mom," she said, realizing that a part of her actually meant it. "Congratulations."

"Thanks! I start on Monday. But today—"

She bent down and reached into the car, then pulled out a square plastic container. "Today I baked cookies for the club meeting. Chocolate chip—your favorite."

*The club meeting.* For a moment all Anna Mei could think of was how good it would feel to just climb into the car with her mother and drive away. No trying to think of something to say about horses, no pretending to be interested in whether the next installment of the Cloverdale Stables series would be as good as the last one.

But the Ponytails were the only friends she had— she couldn't blow them off. And she had a feeling you didn't get any extra chances once you'd made Zoey mad.

"Thanks, Mom," she said. "I'd better get going now."

"Okay. Your dad will pick you up on his way home from work. See you then." Mom slid into the car and started the engine. "Oh, Anna Mei? I wanted to tell you—I think your hair looks cute that way."

Anna Mei reached up self-consciously. She had always worn her straight black hair chin-length, but lately she had been letting it grow. This morning she had managed to scrape it into a short ponytail, with just a fringe of bangs in front.

She looked across to the sidewalk, where Amber, Rachel, and Zoey were waiting for her. "Thanks," she said, then hurried to join them.

# Chapter Eight

# Princess Anna Mei

"What's in there?" Rachel asked, pointing to the plastic container.

"Cookies," Anna Mei said, "for the meeting. I hope you like chocolate chip."

"I like chocolate anything," Amber admitted. "Who doesn't?"

"Come on," Zoey urged them. "We're wasting time." Then, as the girls obediently trotted along beside her, she asked Anna Mei, "Was that your housekeeper?"

It seemed like a weird question. In Boston, no one she knew had a housekeeper. A cleaning lady now and then, maybe. Were housekeepers a normal thing around here?

She shook her head. "No."

"Well, aren't you a little old for a babysitter?" Zoey asked.

"Babysitter?" Anna Mei repeated, still confused. "I don't know what you mean. My mom made these. She wanted us to have them at the meeting."

"Your mom?" Now Zoey seemed confused. "But we thought . . . I mean, aren't your parents Chinese?"

For a moment Anna Mei felt like Dorothy in *The Wizard of Oz*—she kept forgetting she wasn't in Kansas anymore. Back home, everyone had known everything about her. Here, no one had even met her parents yet.

"I was adopted," she said, thinking that would cover the situation.

But Amber didn't see it that way. "Really? Adopted?" She made it sound as if "adopted" meant *dropped on Earth by aliens.* "So you don't even know your real parents?"

"They're not called that," Zoey corrected her. "They're called birth parents. Don't you guys know anything?"

For once Anna Mei was grateful to Zoey for being such a know-it-all. "My birth mother brought me to the orphanage when I was only a few days old," she said. "I don't remember anything about it. Or her."

"An orphanage," Rachel repeated. "That sounds so sad."

"I think it sounds exciting, like something out of a fairy tale!" Amber said, this new and thrilling topic making her imagination work overtime. "It's like . . . *a beautiful but mysterious young woman is forced to flee, leaving her precious daughter behind* . . . You could be a *princess* or something, and not even know it!"

"Oh, come *on,*" Zoey groaned. "I seriously doubt that Anna Mei's a *princess.*"

Anna Mei was feeling more and more uncomfortable with this whole conversation. How much farther was Zoey's house anyway?

"It's really not mysterious at all," she said. "The Chinese government was limiting family size, and since most people wanted boys, a lot of girls ended up in orphanages."

"Is Anna Mei even your real name?" Rachel asked.

"Well, Mei Li was my Chinese name, but my parents wanted to name me after my Grandmother Anna."

Amber, apparently still spinning fantasies in her head, just wouldn't let it go. "They probably couldn't have kids of their own," she announced. "So they traveled far, far from home to find a little baby to raise. It must feel kind of weird for you, though, Anna Mei. I mean, you don't even match your own parents."

When she was younger, Anna Mei's parents had shown her a special box they kept in their bedroom closet, filled with pictures, documents, and mementos of her first few months in China. But it had never really interested her—they were her parents, her life was her life. Why should she care how it had all happened or who she looked like?

But maybe she'd been wrong not to care—these girls certainly did.

"I'm used to it," she said finally, determined to change the subject once and for all. "Just like you're used to having little brothers around."

That finally knocked the smile off Amber's face. "Ugh, don't remind me," she said.

Luckily, Zoey was quickly losing interest in a conversation that didn't revolve around her—or horses. "There's my house," she said, pointing to a white two-story halfway down the block. "I just got a new issue of *Young Rider* and I'm dying to read it."

Only a few moments ago, Anna Mei would have been okay with never hearing about horses again as long as she lived. But if it meant ending the discussion about her strange family, she would talk about them all day long.

"I can't wait," she said, practically sprinting up the sidewalk to Zoey's house.

# Chapter Nine

# One of *These* Things

On Sunday, the Andersons hosted Aunt Karen's family for dinner.

"Look, Aunt Margaret," six-year-old Emily said, holding up the Candy Land card she'd just drawn from the pile. "I got a double purple."

"Hey, you're almost to the Candy Cane Forest," Anna Mei's mother said. "Good job!"

She was sitting at the kitchen table peeling potatoes while Emily and Anna Mei played board games. Aunt Karen was in the living room feeding Benjamin, while Dad and Uncle Jeff had headed to the basement to watch a football game.

"She's already won twice," Anna Mei said. "I think the only way to beat her is to switch to chess."

Emily moved her little gingerbread man carefully

along the colored trail. "But I don't know how to play chess," she pointed out.

"Exactly!" Anna Mei said, grinning at her own joke.

Aunt Karen appeared in the doorway, a drowsy-looking Benjamin in her arms. "What's going on in here?" she asked.

"Mommy!" Emily announced happily. "I'm almost winning!"

"*Again*," Anne Mei said. "I'm thinking of playing Benjamin next time."

"That's silly," Emily told her, frowning at the very idea. "He's only a baby. He doesn't know how to play games."

Anna Mei caught her mother's eye. "Exactly!" they said at the same time, then they both started laughing. Emily, who had no idea what was so funny, just shook her head.

"You're *both* sillies," she informed them, with great seriousness.

"Blurp," Benjamin said, making everyone laugh again.

Aunt Karen said, "Margaret, have I told you how wonderful it is having you here?"

"Only a couple hundred times," Mom answered, as she set the pan of potatoes on the stove and slid a tray of rolls into the oven. "And that's just today."

"Well, I can't help it. I know it hasn't been easy for all of you, leaving your home and your friends, but I just love being able to see you so often. Once or twice a year was never enough."

Anna Mei swallowed hard. She knew Aunt Karen meant well, but the words "it hasn't been easy" didn't begin to cover it.

"Okay, Emily, I give up," she said. "Let's put this away for now. Aunt Karen, could I hold Benjamin for a few minutes?"

"That would be great," her aunt said. "Then I can help your mom with dinner. He's almost asleep anyway."

Aunt Karen shifted the baby into Anna Mei's arms, trying not to rouse him. He felt heavier than she expected, but his hair and skin had a sweet, clean smell she liked. She patted him on the back and murmured softly into his ear.

"Anna Mei, you're a natural," her aunt said approvingly. "I can't wait until you're old enough to start babysitting for me. Come on, Emily, you can help set the table."

Standing in the warm kitchen, her arms full of snuggly, sweet-smelling baby, Anna Mei realized that this house had never seemed cozier. The smell of roasting chicken and warm rolls drifted from the oven. The potatoes bubbled gently on the stove. Mom and Aunt Karen worked side by side, chopping vegetables for the salad and smiling identical smiles. Only two years apart in age, they looked amazingly alike. In fact, so did Emily and Benjamin, with their round cheeks, golden curls, and sky-blue eyes.

Anna Mei felt that tightening in her throat that had been happening more and more lately. It was ridiculous to be jealous of a couple of little kids. But she couldn't help feeling that something was wrong with this picture, and the something was her. It reminded her of that *Sesame Street* game she used to play along with when she was little—the one where you had to decide which thing didn't belong.

Benjamin lifted his head. His eyes met hers as if he might be about to offer a word of comfort or a nugget of wisdom. What he actually did was burp loudly and spit milk all over her shirt.

"Ugh!" Anna Mei cried, all other thoughts flying out of her head.

"Ewwww, gross!" Emily shrieked.

"Hush," Aunt Karen told her, grabbing a clean dish towel for Anna Mei and reaching out to take Benjamin, who'd started to cry. "I'm so sorry," she said. "He hardly ever does that."

"Guess it's my lucky day," Anna Mei said, dabbing at the disgusting glob on her shirt. "I'll go up and change."

"Okay, but don't dawdle," Mom said. "Dinner's almost ready."

"What's *dawdle*?" Emily asked, following Anna Mei to her room. "And why won't Aunt Margaret let you do it?"

In spite of the horrible smell right under her nose, Anna Mei smiled. "It just means we should hurry."

"Oh." Emily seemed disappointed that such an interesting word had such an ordinary explanation. Then her face brightened. "Is Cleo in here?" she asked.

Anna Mei glanced around but didn't see the cat anywhere. "She's probably under the bed. She doesn't like strangers."

"But I'm not a stranger, I'm her cousin," Emily said, with six-year-old logic. "Hey, why do the walls look so funny in here?"

Over the past few weeks, Anna Mei had been pulling off little strips of loose wallpaper. Now spots of turquoise paint peeked out from under the tattered ivy. It looked even worse than before, if that was possible.

"I'm getting it ready to paint," she said, pulling a clean shirt from the drawer.

"Ooh, paint it purple!" Emily urged her. "It's my favorite color."

"Well . . ." Anna Mei hesitated. What color to paint her room had turned out to be a more complicated decision than expected. Her plan to do it all pink with white trim had hit a snag when she had casually mentioned it at Friday's club meeting.

"Pink?" Zoey had said, wrinkling her nose. "Pink is so over, Anna Mei. I already told you that about your shoes, remember? You should paint it lime green. Green is the new pink, you know."

"Lime green with tangerine," Rachel agreed. "I saw that in my mom's decorating magazine. It looked amazing."

"We could help you pick out rugs and pillows and stuff," Amber offered. "Then when it's done we'll have some club meetings at your house."

"Um, thanks," Anna Mei had told them. "I . . . I'll let you know when I'm ready."

Now the sudden appearance of Cleo saved her from having to discuss the subject with Emily, too.

"Hey look, she was in your closet!" Emily said, delighted. She scooped Cleo into her arms. "You're such a nice kitty. I wish I could have a kitty just like you."

"Why can't you?" Anna Mei asked. "Cats are pretty easy to take care of."

Emily buried her face in Cleo's soft belly. "My dad is allergic," she said, her voice muffled. "All we get to have is fish. And they're not all soft and cuddly like you, are they, Cleo?"

Anna Mei stepped into the bathroom to wash up and change her shirt. It occurred to her that maybe things weren't so perfect for Emily after all. As far as she was concerned, all the bouncy blond curls in the world wouldn't make up for not having Cleo.

She was still drying her hands when she heard what sounded like a pack of noisy teenagers stampeding up the stairs. A moment later her mother and aunt burst into the room.

"Dinner's ready!" they sang out in unison, before dissolving into helpless laughter.

Their joy at being together filled up the room, but something stopped Anna Mei from joining in the fun. The way they acted reminded her of how she and Lauren had been. But Lauren was hundreds of miles away.

It seemed so unfair. Why couldn't everyone be happy at the same time?

# Chapter Ten

# *Saturday* Nightmare

Danny held the terrarium up toward the window, peering at the fuzzy stuff inside. Ms. Wagner had given them strict orders not to open the jars—breathing in mold spores could be toxic. But Danny was determined to examine the contents from every possible angle.

"The carrot and potato definitely have the most mold," he said. "The stuff on the cheese is the greenest and also has the most black dots. Are you writing this down?"

Two weeks had passed since they'd started the terrarium experiment, and today was their last chance to observe the results. After this they would throw away the unopened jars and begin writing reports from their notes.

As promised, Danny had stuck Anna Mei with all the note-taking. But after a bumpy start, she had actually enjoyed the project a lot. She thought it was pretty cool of Ms. Wagner to let them do such a unique experiment.

It turned out that not everyone shared her enthusiasm, though. The Ponytails, for example, expressed their distaste at every opportunity. Anna Mei had learned to say little and nod a lot whenever the subject came up. She didn't want everyone thinking she was weird just because she liked science, even the icky parts.

"It looks like the cookie and the taco shell have the least mold," she pointed out. "Those kinds of food have a lot of preservatives, so maybe that's why they stayed fresh longer."

"Hey, that's pretty smart," Danny said. Then, before she could enjoy even this tiniest of compliments, he said, "You're really not like most girls, are you?"

She sighed. Why did everyone in this school seem obsessed with how different she was? She'd been trying for weeks and weeks now to be the *same*. Couldn't they see that?

"And what is that supposed to mean?" she asked him, her voice frosty. "That I'm some kind of freak?"

"No, it means you don't *freak* about this icky stuff. A lot of the girls act like even looking at mold will give them rabies or something."

"Well . . . it's not so bad."

Okay, so maybe it wasn't her wittiest comeback, but it was getting confusing, trying to figure how to act all the time. She'd probably better watch it—if Danny had noticed that she was actually into science, maybe other kids would, too.

"All right, class," Ms. Wagner announced from the front of the room, "now that the observation period is over, make plans with your partner for doing the written report. It should include a chart based on your daily notes, plus your original hypothesis, your results, and your conclusions. The due date is next Wednesday."

Although they'd known about the assignment for weeks, some of the kids groaned anyway, more or less as an automatic reaction to homework assignments in general. Danny, of course, had already come up with a plan to get out of doing it.

"You should write the report," he told Anna Mei. He pulled a sketchbook out of his desk and stuffed it into his backpack. "I'll make the chart and draw a cover. Ours will *look* the best, that's for sure."

"Are you crazy?" Anna Mei asked, although she was pretty sure she already knew the answer to that one. "I'm not going to write the whole report by myself! You have to—"

"Anna Mei!" Zoey had come up behind her. "I just got a new model horse for my collection. Wait until you see all the tack it came with!"

First Danny, and now a Ponytail Club meeting. It was too much for one day.

"Actually, Zoey," she said, "I really, uh, I don't think I can make it today. I'm not feeling very well, probably coming down with something, so . . . I think I'd better go right home."

She was pretty surprised to hear those words coming out of her mouth. They sounded ridiculously lame, even to her, but Zoey just shrugged.

"It's no wonder—anyone would get sick looking at that thing," she said, nodding toward the terrarium on Anna Mei's desk. "I'll be surprised if the whole class doesn't end up in the hospital. Well, I guess you can see the horse next week."

Danny watched her walk away. "Nice talking to you, Zoey," he said to her retreating back. "Bye!"

"Was that rude or what?" he asked Anna Mei, who suddenly felt like she'd just been handed a *Get out of jail free* card. "Because I thought I was standing here, already talking to you. Or have I turned invisible all of a sudden?"

*Don't I wish*, she thought.

———————

Saturday turned out to be one of those perfect mid-October days, crisp and clear, with red and gold trees making sharp outlines against a bright blue sky. Lured outside by the sunshine, Anna Mei had agreed to help her father do some raking. She figured it was one of those jobs that kept you busy but didn't require too much thinking, perfect for someone trying to avoid certain homework assignments.

The yard was bigger than their old one, with a lot more trees, so the lawn was already carpeted in a thick layer of leaves. "I'm going to check the garage for more bags," Dad said after a while. "Having these big piles lying around is just too tempting—I'm afraid I may start jumping in them any minute now."

"Good idea, Dad," she said, pretending to agree. "Let's make sure all our new neighbors know just how dorky you really are, okay?"

"Oh, I get it. Sarcasm, huh? All right, then, you asked for it!" Pretending to take a flying leap into one of the piles, he stopped just in time and disappeared into the garage.

Anna Mei caught herself smiling. She was actually enjoying herself this morning. In fact, maybe she would stay out here all day. After all, that homework would still be waiting for her tomorrow. There was no rush, really, no reason to—

"Hey, Cartoon Girl!"

For a moment she thought she must still be asleep. She'd been dreaming she was raking leaves, and now she was stuck in the middle of some horrible nightmare. It just wasn't possible that Danny Gallagher had escaped from the zoo, or wherever he lived, and was riding his bike into her driveway, grinning like a hyena.

"Looks like you're feeling better," the hyena said, as real as the sun in her eyes and the leaves at her feet.

"Danny, what are you doing here?" she demanded to know. "Does Ms. Wagner give extra credit for bugging me on weekends, too?"

"Is that any way to talk to someone who just wants to see if you're all right?"

She frowned. "What are you talking about?"

"You know—you were sick after school yesterday, remember?"

"Oh . . . right." A sliver of guilt pricked her conscience. She had tried to push the lie out of her mind, telling herself that she'd done it out of self-preservation. It seemed like she'd been saying a lot of things lately that weren't exactly true. But what gave Danny the right to come over here and question her about it?

"Actually, I . . . uh . . . I *am* feeling better," she managed to say. "So . . . I guess you can take off now."

But the bike stayed where it was. "The thing is," Danny said, "there's another reason I stopped by. I was thinking . . ." His voice trailed off and he glanced around the yard as if looking for inspiration. Or possibly cue cards.

Anna Mei realized she had never seen him at a loss for words before. He always acted so sure of himself. What could this be about? She leaned on the rake, waiting.

"Okay, I felt kind of bad about the science report," he finally said. "About telling you to write it by yourself, I mean. It's not that I don't care about it, but I knew it would be a lot better if you did it. I'm pretty bad at writing, to tell you the truth."

She stared at him, too surprised to come up with her usual defensive response. Not only did Danny seem serious, he was acting downright humble. She steeled herself for the punch line that must be coming.

Her father came out of the garage, leaf bags in hand. "I didn't know we had company," he said, extending the other hand to Danny. "I'm Greg Anderson, Anna Mei's dad."

"I'm Danny Gallagher. We're doing a science project together. Me and Anna Mei, I mean."

*Oh, no!* she thought wildly. *Don't tell him that!*

But it was too late. Her father's face had already lit up like a Christmas tree.

"No kidding!" he said, not only shaking Danny's hand, but patting him on the back with so much enthusiasm you'd have thought Albert Einstein himself had just dropped by for a chat. "It's a pleasure to meet you, Danny. I can't wait to hear all about it."

# Chapter Eleven

# Lunch, Anyone?

Danny didn't wait to be asked twice. He immediately launched into a description of mold that was so detailed and so colorful, he made their terrarium sound like the most fascinating science project in the history of science projects. Not that this particular audience needed much convincing.

"That's wonderful!" Anna Mei's father said, his grin even bigger than Danny's. "I can't wait to read your report. Anna Mei must have told you I'm a research scientist."

"Really?" Danny looked over at her with narrowed eyes, almost as if he were accusing her of something. "As a matter of fact, she didn't mention it."

"Well," Anna Mei said loudly, snatching a bag out of Dad's hand. "This yard isn't going to rake itself, you know. We'd better get back to it."

She figured even Danny couldn't miss a giant hint like that. But her father spoke first.

"As if I'd let a few thousand leaves stand in the way of scientific progress," he said. "You two get going on that report, and I'll handle the raking. I'll come in later to rustle up some lunch." He picked up a handful of leaves and scrunched them together. "Get it? Rustle?"

Grinning, Danny climbed off his bike and put the kickstand down. "Come on, Anna Mei, let's make like a tree and leave."

"Oh, good one!" Dad said, and just like that she was trapped. No amount of wishing, no amount of pinching herself to wake up was going to make Danny Gallagher go away. He was here, at her house, and they were going to write a science report together.

"We can use the table in here," she said, leading him through the side door and into the kitchen. "And there's a laptop in my dad's study if we need it."

"Does he work at home?" Danny asked.

"Sometimes, but usually he works at the university. That's where his lab is."

"Really? My dad—" He stopped suddenly, as if he wasn't sure whether he should finish the sentence. A moment later he did. "My dad works there, too. But he's in the maintenance department."

Anna Mei was busy spreading her notes out on the table. Why would he think she'd care where his father worked? All she cared about was getting this report over with. The sooner they did that, the sooner she could get back to avoiding Danny.

"Okay," she said, trying to sound as if this were an ordinary school day and they were not sitting inside her house, at the same table where she ate her breakfast. "We need to start with an introduction, describing what the experiment is and how we set it up."

"But Ms. Wagner already knows all that stuff. Can't we just skip it?"

Anna Mei sighed. This was like trying to explain things to Emily. "No, because a report is supposed to be something anyone could pick up and read without knowing anything about mold. We need to explain that it grows from spores, not seeds like almost everything else. It needs to feed off something to survive."

"Which is where our dinner comes in," Danny said. "The rottener the food, the happier the mold."

"Well . . . yeah," she said, nodding. It wasn't something they could write in the report, of course, but in his own weird way, Danny had gotten it exactly right.

"How about if you draw the cover while I write the introduction?" she suggested. "Then we can both work on the observation part."

"Now you're talking," he said, pulling a sketchpad out of his backpack and flashing that familiar grin.

# Chapter Twelve

# A Different Danny

An hour later they had nearly finished. They had described their procedure and listed all their observations: which foods had gotten moldy first, how many different kinds and colors they saw, which molds had spread from one food to another. They were in the middle of describing how mold spores use chemicals to break down food when Anna Mei's father poked his head in the side door.

"Anyone hungry?" he asked innocently.

Anna Mei and Danny looked up at him, then at each other, then burst out laughing at exactly the same moment.

"Wow, that's the easiest laugh I ever got," he said. "Now maybe you can tell me what's so funny."

"It's just that we were talking about rotting food

and fungi and stuff," Anna Mei explained. "It doesn't exactly make you want to chow down on lunch."

"Why didn't you call me?" he asked, pretending to be hurt. "I'm the most fun-guy I know."

"Ugh, Dad! That's terrible," she groaned, but Danny cracked up.

"At last, someone who appreciates a good joke," Dad said.

"If only you knew any," Anna Mei shot back.

They grinned at each other. It was a familiar, comfortable routine, one they'd been enjoying practically since she could talk. Strange that she didn't feel embarrassed anymore, goofing around with Danny there.

"All right, you two finish up," Dad said, "and I'll come back in a half hour to whip up some sandwiches. Maybe I can get a peek at that report, too," he added.

"I've already got the cover done." Danny held it up to show them. He'd drawn a scary-looking fuzzy green mold monster sneaking up on an unsuspecting slice of bread. Mr. Anderson gave it a thumbs-up before heading back outside.

"Your dad is so cool," Danny said, watching him go. "The way he jokes around with you and wants to know about your school projects. That's really . . ." He seemed to struggle to find the right word, then finally just shrugged.

Anna Mei had never really thought about it before. Didn't all parents care about things their kids did? "I bet you're like that with your dad, too. Being funny probably runs in your family."

She expected him to laugh and say something like, "Are you kidding? In my family it practically gallops!"

But he didn't answer at all. Instead he seemed suddenly intent on fine-tuning his drawing, adding even more detail to the monster's jagged eyebrows. Without looking up he said, "My dad has to work a lot of nights. When he comes home he doesn't feel much like joking, I guess."

"Oh. Well . . ." her voice trailed off. She was sorry she'd gotten into this conversation in the first place. It made her feel uncomfortable to see Danny this way, so different from his happy-go-lucky-yet-irritating self. She was relieved when he finally looked up from his sketch.

"Perfect," he decided. "Between your writing and my drawing, we'll have the best report in the whole class."

"You helped with the writing, too," she said. She hated to admit it, but fair was fair. "You had some really good ideas and observations."

"Yeah, but you made them sound a lot better. I'm glad Ms. Wagner made us partners."

Was this really Danny talking? The boy who'd

been picking on her since the first day she set foot in room 117?

She started gathering up her notes, buying time to think about how to answer. But he didn't wait for an answer. "You know, I've been wanting to ask you something," he said.

Anna Mei sighed. She should have known those compliments weren't sincere. Now he was going to ask her to do his English homework for him, or maybe help him with math. "Because you're so good at it," he'd say, all full of phony charm.

But what he actually said was, "Why didn't you want to go to that horse thing yesterday? At Zoey's house?"

She was so startled she couldn't think fast enough to deny it. The truth flew out of her mouth before she could stop it.

"I don't really like horses," she heard herself say. "I only go to the meetings because . . ."

What was she thinking, confessing this to *Danny*, of all people? It would just give him more ammunition.

"Because why?"

She might as well get it over with. "Because they asked me," she said. "Zoey and Amber and Rachel, I mean. I didn't care what the club was—I just wanted to have some friends."

Danny snorted. "You call those friends? A bunch of horsey-tails with their noses in the air?"

"*Pony*tails," she corrected him, suddenly glad she wasn't wearing one at the moment.

He waved his hand dismissively, as if she was missing the whole point. "Whatever," he said. "I'm just saying, there are lots of kids you could be friends with, if you'd stop hanging around with the snobby ones."

That was too much, coming from him.

"*You're* criticizing *them*?" she demanded, her voice rising. "When you've done nothing but insult me ever since I got here?"

Either he was genuinely surprised or he was the best actor she'd ever seen. "Insult you?" he repeated. "What are you talking about?"

"You call me Cartoon Girl!" She was practically shouting now. How dense could he be?

Danny's eyes widened. "But that's a compliment," he said.

"Oh, right," she said, her voice lower but heavy with sarcasm. "Sure it is."

"No, really," he insisted. "I'm a huge cartoon fan. I love anime and manga. Look . . ."

He started flipping through his sketchbook, showing her all his drawings of Japanese-style cartoons—page after page of dashing heroes, big-eyed creatures, and menacing monsters.

"I just think it's cool that your name sounds the same," he told her. "It's different."

Anna Mei kept her eyes on his sketchbook, not trusting herself to speak. "Different" was exactly what she was trying so hard to avoid.

"I didn't know it bothered you," Danny said then. "Why didn't you just tell me?"

When she finally opened her mouth to answer, she realized that she didn't *have* an answer. Why *hadn't* she just told him? On her very first day at Elmwood, Zoey and the other girls had said he was a jerk, that he was always saying stupid things and bothering people. She had figured they knew what they were talking about. And when they'd invited her to be a Ponytail, well, it had seemed easiest just to go along.

It was kind of a lame reason, she realized now, but it was all she had. "I guess I should have told you," she said finally. "I thought you were picking on me because I was new, or because I'm Chinese, or something."

"What?" Danny looked genuinely exasperated. "Who cares about any of that stuff?"

"You don't know what it's—" she began, then stopped when her father came back into the room.

"I don't know about you, but I'm starving," he said, brushing a leaf out of his hair. "Besides, I can't wait to find out what the mold monster did to the poor defenseless bread."

# Chapter Thirteen

# Just a Little White Lie

The next week seemed to pass in a frenzy of activity. Everything at school revolved around the carnival—officially called the Fall Follies—coming up on Friday.

The sixth graders in all three homerooms spent part of every afternoon creating decorations. They made huge poster board signs for the games and activities, plus construction paper leaves, bats, and spiders to hang from the ceiling. Disappointed to discover that bringing real straw into the building would violate fire codes, they hit on the idea of making fake scarecrows by stuffing old clothes with newspapers and using paper bags for the heads. These would be posed at the entrances and scattered around the gym for atmosphere. The finishing touches—real pumpkins—were being donated by a local grocery store.

Anna Mei liked all the hustle and bustle. For one thing, it kept her mind off things she'd rather ignore. Things like her heritage report, which she hadn't started working on, even though hardly a day went by without Ms. Wagner reminding them that November was just around the corner.

Another plus to all the carnival activity was that she'd found herself spending time with classmates she hadn't talked with much before. Working on projects with kids like Luis and Zandra, she'd started to join in their conversations about how boring math class had been lately and which TV shows were starting to get really good.

On Wednesday, the three of them were cutting out paper leaves and threading them on fishing line when Zandra said, "Oh, I wanted to tell you guys—my parents said I could have some kids over before the carnival. You know, just to help each other with our costumes and makeup and stuff. Want to come?"

"I have to watch my little sisters until my mom gets home from work," Luis said, "but I'll see if she can bring me over after that."

"I have to—I mean, I already have plans," Anna Mei told her. "Thanks for asking, though."

It had been a pleasant surprise to be included in Zandra's invitation. Maybe there was hope that her "new kid" label was starting to fade a little. Maybe Danny hadn't been completely crazy after all.

Danny. He'd left on Saturday, finally, after eating two grilled cheese sandwiches and chatting with Anna Mei's dad for what seemed like forever.

"So did you enjoy this project?" Dad asked him, after reading their report. "I would have loved it when I was your age. Of course, mold hadn't been invented yet, way back then."

Danny grinned. "It was fun," he said, "especially since I didn't have to do much of the writing. I can never seem to make the words come out on paper like they sound in my head."

"Well, people have different talents," Dad said, sounding serious for a change. "I was never much of a writer myself, but I learned to be better at it when I realized it would help me do what I loved—study science."

"I already know what I love," Danny said, gathering up his sketchpad and pencils. "Cartooning. I'm planning to be ready the day an animation studio calls me. But you've given me a great idea, Mr. Anderson—I think I'll dress up like a mad scientist for the Follies. How does that sound, Anna Mei?"

"Like a perfect fit," she'd answered, rolling her eyes.

The whole situation was confusing, even annoying. All these weeks she'd thought she had

Danny all figured out—he was the class clown, the goof-off, the kid who was all mouth and no brains.

But for some reason he seemed determined to break out of that box, the one she had neatly labeled *Trouble*. He had worked hard on their report. He had been polite—even charming—with her father. Next thing you knew he'd be helping little old ladies cross the street.

"You've all done a wonderful job on these decorations," Ms. Wagner was saying now. "I know the parent council will be very pleased. I want you to enjoy the Follies tonight and Halloween tomorrow, so I won't be giving any homework over the weekend."

Spontaneous cheers and high-fives popped out all over the room.

"However," Ms. Wagner continued, and the cheers froze on their lips. Eyes wide, breath held, they waited for whatever medieval torture she was about to inflict. "I have finished grading your science reports, and because you worked so hard on them, I wanted to hand them back today."

Relief filled up the room like helium escaping from twenty-four balloons. Ms. Wagner walked up and down the aisles, handing out reports and murmuring congratulations.

"Danny, Anna Mei, excellent work," she said as she reached the back of the room. "I didn't want to mark on your imaginative drawing, so I put your grade inside." She pulled back the cover page to show them the bright red A.

"Wow!" Danny said, his eyes bright, his smile wide. "I guess we make a good team, Cartoon—er, Anna Mei. Do you want to hang out at the Follies tonight? It was cool of your dad to lend me a lab coat—I want to show him how my costume turned out."

"Um, actually, I'm, well . . ." Anna Mei stammered. Ugh. What was her *problem* lately? She'd made plans to go with the Ponytails—why couldn't she just say so? Why should she care what Danny thought? "Amber's giving me a ride," she finally managed to say. "And my parents aren't coming. They . . . both have to work tonight."

"That's too bad," he said. "Your dad seems like the kind of guy who really gets into Halloween."

"Yeah," Anna Mei said lamely. She got busy fiddling with her backpack, hoping Danny wouldn't notice how flushed her face suddenly looked. Really, all this lying was getting out of control.

The truth was she hadn't even invited her parents. She hadn't wanted to face the surprised stares when she walked into the gym with two blond giants towering over her. So first she had told Ms. Wagner that both her parents had to work tonight. Then she'd convinced her parents that the carnival was only for students.

It had seemed better for everyone, really. She'd been sure it was the right decision . . . and yet she couldn't shake the feeling that she had somehow betrayed them.

Plus Danny had nailed it—her father was *exactly* the kind of guy who loved Halloween. When she was little he'd always dressed up in a goofy costume to take her trick-or-treating around the neighborhood. When she got too old for that, he'd worn a scary mask to hand out candy to the other kids, greeting most of them by name and admiring all their costumes, no matter how dopey. He'd probably have shown up tonight in a werewolf outfit, then stayed to play every game and sample every treat.

*I'm sorry, Dad*, Anna Mei told him silently, guiltily.

At least the Ponytails had agreed to skip their meeting tonight, so they'd have plenty of time to get ready for the carnival. These days, it seemed, Anna Mei had to take small blessings wherever she could find them.

# Chapter Fourteen

# *Fatal* Phone Call

*C*lomp. *Thud. Crash.*

She'd never be the most graceful cowgirl on the range, that's for sure. How did anyone walk in these silly boots anyway, let alone wrangle ponies? Or whatever cowgirls did with ponies.

"What's going on up there?" her father called from the living room. "Are you hiding a herd of elephants in your bedroom?"

Anna Mei managed to make it down the stairs, clomping all the way and sending a frightened Cleo skittering out of her path. "I'm just having a little trouble with these boots," she explained. "Amber let me borrow them, but they're way too big for me."

"Well, turn around, li'l lady," Dad said in a fake drawl, setting his newspaper aside. "Let's see how you look."

She already knew how she looked—absolutely ridiculous. Who dressed up like a cowgirl for Halloween? No one over the age of five, that's who.

But Zoey had insisted. "No monster stuff," she'd announced. "We'll all wear chaps with fringe, plus leather boots and our best hats. Everyone will be able to tell who the Ponytails are."

That part was probably true. Anna Mei was pretty sure no one would confuse them with a punk rock band or a troupe of ballerinas.

"So this is all borrowed finery?" her father asked while she did the pirouette thing for him. She nodded. Of course, it was probably only a matter of time before she'd have to start buying some of this stuff for herself. No self-respecting Ponytail would be caught dead without the latest in leather chaps.

"Very nice," he pronounced, with underwhelming enthusiasm. "Not exactly as creative as the costumes you usually come up with . . . but nice."

Anna Mei shrugged. It was true—in past years she'd concocted everything from a two-headed alien to a polka-dot pterodactyl. But that was when all that mattered was having fun. Back then she'd had nothing to lose.

"It's so everyone in the club matches," she told him.

"Ah," he said, which she'd learned was his version of *whatever*. "And are you sure you don't need a ride?"

"Amber's parents are picking me up," she said, then quickly added, "and dropping us off at school." In fact, Amber's parents would be staying to help at the refreshment booth, but Anna Mei's father didn't need to know that.

"Okay, but wait a minute while I get the camera," he said. "Your mom was disappointed that she has to work tonight, so I promised her I'd take your picture."

Anna Mei flopped down on the couch. Cleo, who'd taken refuge under there, yowled at the intrusion.

"Sorry, Cleo, it's just me. Don't you recognize me?" Cleo poked her head out but refused to be coaxed into Anna Mei's lap. "I don't blame you," she told the cat, "I hardly recognize myself lately."

Before she could ponder this unexpected observation, the phone rang. Her father picked it up in his study, where he'd gone in search of the camera. She wished he would hurry—she needed to scoot out the door as soon as Amber arrived, so that the parents wouldn't have a chance to compare notes.

"Yes, I understand," she heard him say. "Well, as it turns out, I am available and I'd be happy to help. Just give me a few details."

Good, it sounded like he might actually have to go the lab for a while. Well, not good for *him*, of course, but at least it meant both of her parents really *were* working tonight. She didn't have to feel so bad about keeping them away from the carnival.

He finally returned, camera in hand. Anna Mei sprang up from the couch, then winced as she turned her ankle in the heavy boot.

"Can we please hurry, Dad? Amber's parents will be here any second, and you know how parents hate to be kept waiting." She figured it didn't hurt to appeal to his sense of parental unity.

"Actually," he answered, setting the camera down on the coffee table, "it appears that you and I need to have a little chat before you go."

"But I—" she started, then caught sight of his face. It had lost all signs of the earlier playfulness. "What's wrong?"

"That was someone on the parent council at school," he said. "Apparently there have been some cancellations from parents who were scheduled to work at the carnival tonight. They're looking for last-minute replacements."

"Oh," she said, in a voice so small she could have been mistaken for an *actual* five-year-old cowgirl. She made an effort to pump it up a little. "Yeah, I guess a few parents were coming, just to help out. You know, so the teachers wouldn't be stuck doing it all."

"According to the woman I just talked to, quite a few parents will be helping out. Not to mention all those who will be attending as guests. But she somehow had the impression that your mom and I were unavailable. Any idea how that might have happened?"

Anna Mei's legs suddenly felt wobbly, as if they'd both decided to take the night off and would be unavailable for a while themselves. She sank back down on the couch and waited. It was so quiet she could hear the clock on the wall behind her, ticking off the seconds. Then the minutes. Finally her gut sent a message to her brain: *Tell the truth.*

"I'm sorry, Dad," she said, looking down at the floor instead of at him. It was the only way she could get the words out. "I know I shouldn't have told Ms. Wagner that you and Mom couldn't come. It's just . . ."

He waited as more seconds ticked by. She had to force the rest out in a rush. "Well, anyone who sees us together can tell I'm adopted. I mean, it's obvious. So I thought if you didn't go to the carnival, people wouldn't know. And I wouldn't seem so . . . different."

"Different from . . .?" he prompted.

"From everyone!" she said. Why couldn't he see it? "Come on, Dad—no one else in my class is Chinese, or adopted. I hate being the weird one."

"Since when does being Chinese and adopted make you weird?" he asked. "It never seemed to bother you before."

"I was never the new kid before," she said simply.

Her father seemed to let this sink in. Then he said slowly, "I guess I didn't realize how hard this move has been on you, Anna Mei. Your mom and I were sure you wouldn't have any trouble making friends."

Anna Mei's heart sank right down to her oversize boots. She couldn't understand how everything had gone so wrong. She hadn't wanted to move here in the first place, hadn't asked to have to start over at a new school and make new friends. But she was trying—couldn't anyone see that? So how had it ended up with that hurt look on her father's face, and his voice coming out all sad? She had to fight the urge to fall sobbing into his arms, just like she'd done when she was little and had broken a favorite toy or skinned her knee.

"It's okay, Dad," she said. "I should have told you about the carnival. Maybe we could—"

Headlights swept across the room as a car pulled up outside. A short blast on the horn meant Amber's family had arrived.

"You go on," her father said. "I agreed to help with a game, but I'm going to change my clothes and leave a message for your mom first."

"What about the picture?" she asked, in a last attempt to turn back the clock and erase that look from her father's eyes.

"We'll take it afterward," he said. "Go ahead."

"Okay. Bye, Dad," she said, managing to get herself off the couch and over to the door.

But at the last minute she clomped back to give him the hug she'd been holding inside since the phone call.

"I'm glad you're coming," she told him, and meant it. Mostly, anyway.

# Chapter Fifteen

# The *Fall* Follies

"I can't believe how great it all looks!" Amber said. She had to raise her voice to be heard above the noise.

The girls were standing near the refreshment stand, sipping apple cider and snacking on orange-frosted cupcakes dotted with candy corn.

Zoey sighed. "You've said that, like, a hundred times already."

Anna Mei kept quiet, but secretly she agreed with Amber—the transformation of the gym was amazing. Multicolored leaves and black spiders twirled above their heads, suspended on invisible fishing line. Cafeteria tables arranged to form game booths were draped with black tablecloths and strung with twinkling orange lights. The raggedy scarecrows they'd worked so hard to make were scattered around the room, surrounded by fat pumpkins and potted mums. Even the basketball hoops had been draped with twists of black and orange crepe paper.

Judging from the size of the crowd—and the noise level—everyone in the whole school must have turned out. Martians mixed with mummies while pirates stood shoulder to shoulder with princesses, all handing over their tickets for a chance to pop balloons with darts, toss rings at soda bottles, and fish for prizes in a big plastic wading pool.

There was no dance room or dunk tank, much to Zoey's disappointment. But they did have music coming in over the P.A. system, and the games so far had been pretty fun. The best one, they all agreed, was the haunted house set up in the locker room underneath the gym. The Ponytails hadn't expected to be frightened—after all, they weren't little kids anymore, and they'd changed clothes in here about a million times.

But in the dark, the familiar room became a labyrinth of unexpected twists and turns. A silent escort, dressed in ghostly white, used his flashlight sparingly, illuminating a vampire's coffin here or a bubbling cauldron there. Sounds of creaking floors, eerie moans, and howling wind floated through the room, along with a steady *drip, drip, drip*. Silky webs dangled from the ceiling and brushed against their faces. And when a dark figure jumped out of the shadows with a blood-curdling cry, they all screamed and crashed into each other trying to reach the exit.

They had needed the refreshments to regroup. "So what haven't we done yet?" Zoey asked now, tossing her empty cup into a trash can.

"I see a few more games over there," Rachel reported, pointing to the opposite corner of the gym.

Anna Mei took a deep breath. Since they hadn't run into him yet, her father must be working at one of those booths. She'd decided to just act casual about the whole thing, use the "Oh hi, Dad, fancy meeting you here" approach. After all, the Ponytails already knew she was adopted, and probably no one else would figure out who he was anyway.

They threaded their way through the crowd, trying not to mow down any little kids or step on anyone's tail. Finally Anna Mei spotted her father at a booth called *Shake, Rattle and Roll.*

"Step right up, make the skeletons dance!" he was saying to a group of kids passing by. "Just two tickets are all it takes."

To Anna Mei's relief, he hadn't worn a costume after all. He'd only topped a pair of khakis with a denim shirt, then added a jack-o'-lantern tie. It was pretty tame, for him.

"Do you know why the skeleton didn't cross the road?" they heard him ask a little boy dressed like a football player. "Because he didn't have the guts!"

The boy giggled. So did Amber. "That's cute," she said.

Anna Mei took a deep breath. It was now or never. "That's . . . my dad," she said. And in the understatement of the year, added: "He likes corny jokes."

"Well, come on," Zoey said, "let's try the game."

There was no turning back now. Cowboy hat dangling down her back, ponytail swinging behind her, Anna Mei stepped forward to introduce her friends to her father.

# Chapter Sixteen

# Shake, Rattle and Roll

He looked up and saw them coming. "Well, I declare," he said, in a fake cowboy accent. "If it isn't a whole passel of purty cowgirls. Good evening, ladies."

"Hi, Dad," Anna Mei said, maybe a little too heartily. She dialed it back a bit. "These are my friends—Zoey, and Rachel, and Amber."

"Otherwise known as the Ponytail Club, I believe. I'm very happy to meet you all," he said. "Are you having a good time?"

"Yeah, it's pretty cool," Amber said. "We played a lot of games already."

"Ah, but you haven't played the best game of all. I refer, of course, to *Shake, Rattle and Roll.*"

This game featured a row of plastic skeletons

dangling from long strings. Six of the skeletons were small, three were medium-size, and one was huge. But with all the strings gathered together and threaded through a single small ring, it was impossible to tell which string was attached to which skeleton.

"All you have to do is pull on one of these strings to win a prize. But the bigger the skeleton, the bigger the prize. Come on, give it a try."

Ever the fearless leader, Zoey stepped forward.

"By the way," Dad said, while Zoey tore two tickets from the bunch in her pocket, "Did you hear why the skeleton didn't go to the dance?"

Zoey looked at him, her face blank. "Well . . . um . . . no?"

He hit her with the punch line. "Turns out the poor guy had no body to dance with. No body at all."

Anna Mei braced herself for the sarcastic remark she was sure would follow, but Zoey just smiled while the other girls giggled. The string Zoey picked made one of the medium-size skeletons dance, earning her a key chain with two tiny dice attached.

Rachel ended up pulling on a small skeleton, as did Anna Mei, earning them each a candy necklace. Amber couldn't decide which string to choose. She had one in her hand, then at the last minute tugged on a different one. When the biggest skeleton jumped up, she squealed with delight.

"I told you, best game at the carnival," Dad said,

handing her a small furry pillow with a peace sign stitched on the front.

Amber stroked the purple fur. "Thanks," she said, her face beaming. "This will look great in my room."

"So where are you ladies headed next?" Dad asked.

"Well, we haven't entered the raffle yet," Rachel said. "They have a lot of good prizes—I can't decide which ones to buy tickets for."

"I like that manicure set," Zoey said. "I could use some new nail polish."

"I want those free music downloads," Amber said.

"I'll tell you what," Dad said, reaching into his back pocket and pulling out his wallet. He handed Anna Mei a five-dollar bill. "Tickets are a quarter apiece, right? Now you can each enter five times— my treat."

Chiming in with the other girls to thank him, Anna Mei felt herself relax a little. In spite of what had happened earlier, her father seemed to be acting like his old self. And the girls seemed to like him. Maybe she'd been silly to worry about what people would think. Maybe everything would be just—

"Hey, Mr. A.!"

Anna Mei closed her eyes and sighed. She didn't need to look—she'd know that voice anywhere.

"Well, if it isn't Dan the Man," she heard her father say. "At least, I think it is. There's something a little different about you tonight . . . something I can't quite put my finger on . . ."

Danny came over to join the girls, who appeared to be struck speechless at the sight of him. He was a sight to behold, all right—a "mad scientist" who tested the very limits of that term. The lab coat Mr. Anderson had loaned him was covered with plastic flies and spiders. An oversized test tube filled with disgusting green goo hung from a cord around his neck. His hair, spray-painted in purple and red streaks, had been gelled to within an inch of its life so that it stuck out in spikes all over his head. The enormous black glasses that sat precariously on his freckled nose were topped with fuzzy caterpillar eyebrows, while his face was dotted with fake oozing scabs.

Even as she worried about what might happen next, Anna Mei felt a little stab of jealousy. It was exactly the kind of costume she would have dreamed up herself, once.

"Not bad," her father said. "But I don't see what's so crazy about it. I pretty much look like that every day."

Danny grinned. "Thanks for lending me the lab coat, Mr. A. I promise to return it safe and sound."

"Bring it by the house any time," Dad said, going so far as to pat Danny on his bug-covered shoulder. "You're always welcome."

Even without looking their way, Anna Mei knew the girls were staring at her. She smiled weakly, hoping that would leave things open to interpretation, and tried desperately to think of a way to get the Ponytails to hit the trail.

Her father was no help. "So Danny," he said, "how about trying your luck against my incredibly spooky skeletons? Amber just won a grand prize."

"Sounds good," Danny said, plunking his tickets down on the table. "Hey, that reminds me—do you know why skeletons aren't afraid of the police?"

"No," Dad said, as if they were a comedy team and had rehearsed in advance. "Why aren't skeletons afraid of the police?"

"Because no one can ever pin anything on them."

Her father roared with laughter. Zoey, Amber, and Rachel exchanged pained glances. And Anna Mei silently wished for a huge hole to open in the gym floor, one big enough to swallow her without a trace. But of course she never had luck like that.

"So . . . Danny comes over to your house?" Zoey asked, in a voice that sounded like she'd just stepped in dog poo. A voice loud enough for all of them to hear.

Anna Mei found herself resorting to her old standby: stammering. "Well, no . . . I mean . . . no, of course not. We had to work on that terrarium project once, but that was for school."

She didn't actually say the words "we're not friends or anything," but they hung there in the air, like fog curling around her head. The girls nodded, their expressions a mixture of relief and sympathy. Everyone knew that a school assignment, however repulsive, was nothing a mere student could control.

But Danny wasn't nodding. In fact, his expression was one Anna Mei had already seen once tonight— only the first time it had been on her father's face.

"Come on, let's go look at those raffle prizes," Zoey said. "Thanks again for the tickets, Mr. Anderson."

"Yeah, thanks," Rachel and Amber echoed.

"Bye, Dad," Anna Mei said, in a pretend cheerful voice that made her feel sick inside. She risked a glance at Danny, but he had turned away.

# Chapter Seventeen

# November
## *Arrives*

When all the figures had been tallied, the carnival was deemed a huge success, yielding higher attendance and bigger profits than anyone had hoped for. The parent council was promising an even better version next year.

Anna Mei had returned her borrowed outfit immediately, turning down an invitation to go trick-or-treating with the Ponytails on Saturday. She already had more candy than she could possibly eat, she told them, and besides, her parents were counting on her to help give out candy at home. Then she'd told her parents she was too tired to help, and spent the evening watching an old Dracula movie in the basement.

At Mass on Sunday, the familiar hymns and prayers Anna Mei had heard all her life flowed around her. But the words didn't penetrate the cocoon of hopelessness that seemed to surround her. During the Scripture readings, she didn't follow along in the missal as she usually did. It took all her concentration to keep pushing away the memories from carnival night, memories she wanted to lock away forever.

She closed her eyes as Father Mark took his spot on the altar steps, where he liked to give his homily. If she could just get through the next half hour, maybe she could come up with some excuse to spend the rest of the day in her room. Or maybe at the library. Then she could—

"And what a day for celebration!" The excitement in Father Mark's voice broke into Anna Mei's thoughts. She opened her eyes to see him gesturing toward the whole congregation. "Each and every one of us has a reason to rejoice today."

Celebrate? Rejoice? He wasn't talking about *her*, that's for sure.

"Today's readings assure us that we're all God's children, and that he loves us just as any parent loves his child—deeply and forever. As Saint John tells us in the second reading, God has a special plan for each of us, and even if that plan isn't clear yet, we have to trust that it will bring us closer to him in the end."

*Maybe God's plan for me was to be in this family,* Anna Mei thought. *Maybe I was supposed to end up in this place, and I'm here for a reason. But I don't know what it is. I don't know what I'm supposed to do now, or even who I'm supposed to be. I just feel . . . lost.*

⁓

With the carnival over and no more plans or decorations to make, it was back to business as usual in room 117. And a week later, the moment Anna Mei had been dreading since her first day at Elmwood Elementary had finally arrived: it was time for the heritage reports to begin.

Ms. Wagner had drawn names at random and assigned due dates. So from now until Thanksgiving, two students a day would stand in front of the class with their props and their ethnic foods, describing what they'd learned about their family history.

Anna Mei's date would be next Monday. She'd tried, over and over, to imagine what she would say, but it always came out something like this: "My father is Swedish and my mother is Danish, but I'm neither. I was born in China to parents I never met and don't know anything about. The end." It would be the shortest report in the history of oral reports, a real *Guinness World Records* award-winner. Ms. Wagner would probably have to assign some extra homework just to fill up the class time.

She'd actually thought about asking Ms. Wagner for help, but then decided it was too risky. What if her teacher just nodded sympathetically and said,

"Certainly, Anna Mei, since you obviously have no family history whatsoever, you may be excused from this assignment"? Anna Mei might as well just write the word *freak* across her forehead.

Part of her longed to go to her parents for advice, something she'd always been able to do before. But things were so weird with them lately. Ever since the night of the Follies, it felt like they were all tiptoeing around one another, trying not to do or say anything upsetting.

Anna Mei kept wanting to push the memory of that night into a little box that she never had to open again. She wanted to forget how nice her father had been, even after she'd tried to ditch him. And most of all, she wanted to forget how Danny had looked when, instead of sticking up for him, she'd turned her back and slunk away.

One night, she had heard her parents talking in the kitchen, thinking she was upstairs in bed.

"She was worried about people thinking our family was weird, because she wasn't born to us," Dad was saying. "I never realized how much that bothered her."

"I don't think it ever did before," Mom told him. "We always encouraged her to talk about being adopted, and how she felt about it, but she never wanted to."

"I'm sure there are other adopted kids at the school," Dad said, "but she seems to think it's important somehow. Maybe we should have prepared her better for the questions people might ask. Kids are naturally curious, after all."

Mom sighed deeply. "Maybe I was being selfish, wanting us to move here. I just thought . . . being close to our family seemed like the best thing for all of us. But now I don't know."

How had everything gone so wrong? Tears stinging her eyes, Anna Mei had tiptoed back upstairs and pretended to read until her mother came to say good night.

As for Danny . . . Danny hadn't even spoken to her since the Follies. All week long he sat at his desk, doing his schoolwork or sketching, avoiding her the same way she used to avoid him. A few weeks ago she would have thought she'd found paradise. To her shock, she discovered she missed his constant chatter and cheerful attitude. She even missed his dumb jokes.

One day, Ms. Wagner had kept Danny in at recess. Some of the kids teased him, assuming Danny was in trouble for something. But Anna Mei thought Ms. Wagner might be worried about him. Maybe she missed the old Danny, too.

Now Ms. Wagner was announcing that heritage reports would begin. Luis, who had drawn lucky number 1, marched up to the front of the room. He was carrying a plate of cookies and wearing a brightly colored striped blanket over his shoulder.

"*¡Hola!*" he began enthusiastically. "*Me llamo* Luis Hernandez, and my ancestors on my father's side came from Mexico."

Thousands of years ago, Luis explained, great Indian civilizations built pyramids and huge cities in Mexico. Then in the 1500s, the Spanish conquered Mexico, and the two races began to mix. Today, most Mexicans consider themselves *mestizos,* meaning they have both Indian and European ancestors.

Luis's great-grandfather grew up in a small village in the Yucatan Peninsula. He came to America during World War II, when laborers were needed to work in the weapons factories. Later, Luis's grandfather moved to Michigan to work on the General Motors assembly line. The blanket Luis was wearing, called a *serape*, had once belonged to his grandfather.

"A few years ago my family visited Mexico," he said. "Lots of my Hernandez cousins still live near the same place where my great-grandfather grew up."

"Very nice, Luis," Ms. Wagner said. "Can you tell us about the food you brought in?"

"Well, I figured everybody already knows about tacos and enchiladas," he said, "so I asked my mother to help me make some *biscochitos*—sugar cookies."

The class applauded Luis's presentation and gave a unanimous thumbs-up to the cookies.

Elizabeth's turn was next. "My mother's family is from Austria," she began. "And if you've ever seen the movie *The Sound of Music*, you know how beautiful it is there."

Anna Mei remembered that movie—it was one of her mother's favorites. There weren't any orphanages in it, that's for sure.

# Chapter Eighteen

# Lucky Charms

The heritage reports continued all week long. Anna Mei wished she could relax and enjoy them—they really were pretty interesting. The family stories were so different from one another, and yet all these kids had ended up in this one classroom in Michigan. So many cultures had come together here—no wonder America was called "the melting pot."

On Friday, Zandra's report was first. One of her relatives had traced the family back to Cameroon, on the West Coast of Africa. For centuries, a tribe called the Tikar lived there, developing their own government, industry, and art. But because they were surrounded by nothing but grassy savannas and plains, they were easy targets when the slave traders came in the 1800s.

So when Zandra's ancestors came to America, it wasn't by choice. She didn't know what had happened to all of them, but at least a few had been able to escape to Canada. Eventually, some had moved to Michigan to work in the logging camps, and Zandra's great-grandfather was one of them.

"My uncle visited Cameroon once," she said. "He let me borrow this to show you—it's a hand-carved Tikar tribal mask. I really hope to go there myself someday, so I can see the places my ancestors lived."

Then it was Danny's turn. Bringing his backpack with him to the front of the room, he first made a big show of putting on a green plastic top hat and a white vest with huge shamrocks all over it.

"*Dia dhuit*," he said. "That's Gaelic for *hello*. My mother's name was O'Connor, so I'm Irish on both sides, which probably explains the red hair and freckles. Now, you may think you already know a lot about Ireland. For example—"

He reached into his backpack and pulled out a box of cereal. "A lot of you probably think it's all about leprechauns, those wee folk who go around hiding pots of gold." In a corny Irish accent, he mimicked the line from the commercial: "Always after me Lucky Charms."

After the laughter died down he went on. "Or you might think that everyone there goes crazy on Saint Patrick's Day, step dancing through the town square and kissing the Blarney Stone."

Suddenly he yanked off the hat and vest, tossing them on the floor. "Well, I'm here to tell you, there's a lot more to being Irish than that fake stuff!"

Then Danny talked about the great clans who had lived on the Emerald Isle long ago, divided into dozens of small kingdoms called *tuaths*. In 1800, Ireland united with England, Wales, and Scotland to form a new country—the United Kingdom. Then in the 1840s, hunger and disease devastated Ireland. Before the famine ended, hundreds of thousands of people had died.

In order to survive, the Gallagher family had left their home in Galway, joining more than a million and a half Irish who emigrated to America. They spread across the country, helping build the bridges, railroads, and canals that linked Americans to one another.

"My mother's family survived the famine, and some of them still live there," Danny explained. "These days, Ireland has made a great comeback. It's really beautiful, and a lot of tourists go there because they want to visit the place where their ancestors lived."

He held up one of the items he'd brought from home. "This is a piece of Irish lace that belonged to my Grandmother O'Connor. And this was her Bible. It has a bunch of family dates written inside, plus a blessing my mother used to read to me. It's kind of like wishing something good for someone you care about:

Walls for the wind,
A roof for the rain,
And tea beside the fire.
Laughter to cheer you,
Those you love near you,
And all that your heart may desire.

Finally, he adopted the tone of a politician about to make a serious and important point. "So the moral of my report is this: Ireland—Way More Than Just Leprechauns."

The class broke into spontaneous applause. Ms. Wagner joined in, smiling her approval and inviting Danny to share the Irish soda bread he'd brought in. "It's from a bakery," he admitted, "but they promised me it was good."

He walked around the room, breaking chunks off the loaf and handing them out. When he got to Anna Mei, she told him, "I really liked your report, Danny. You're a much better writer than you think."

He paused for just a moment, then said "thanks" before moving on, all without meeting her eyes.

It wasn't exactly a conversation, but it was a start. Rome wasn't built in a day and all that.

Later, while everyone was getting ready for dismissal, Zoey stopped by Anna Mei's desk. "Are you bringing anything to the meeting today? Amber has some new posters she bought online."

Anna Mei sighed. Friday used to be her favorite

day of the week—when had she started to dread it? She'd joined the Ponytail Club thinking she'd make some friends and have some fun. Now here she was almost three months later, still waiting for the fun part to kick in.

"You know, Zoey," she heard herself saying, "I don't think I can make it today. I have things to do at home."

No stammering, no lame excuses. For once the words came out of her mouth just the way they had sounded in her head.

Zoey was looking at her with irritation, a look Anna Mei had seen many times before. For some reason, it didn't bother her this time. "Well, you know you're supposed to reserve Fridays for meetings," Zoey said, in her lecturing tone. "Ponytails is important. And you still haven't taken a turn hosting."

"I know," Anna Mei said, hoping she sounded sincerely regretful. "I'll catch you next week."

In a stroke of the luck that rarely seemed to come Anna Mei's way, the dismissal bell rang right at that moment. Zoey hurried off to find Amber and Rachel, probably so she could report on what a disappointment a certain club member was turning out to be.

It wasn't until Anna Mei turned to grab her backpack that she realized Danny was standing there and that he'd been listening the whole time.

# Chapter Nineteen

# "My Daughter, Mei Li"

She had planned to sleep in on Saturday, preferably as late as possible. Sleep offered at least some kind of protection against the constant worry about her report, not to mention the humiliation of being graded a big fat zero on Monday. But she must have forgotten to alert her subconscious, because a bad dream nudged her rudely awake just before dawn.

Her room was still pretty dark, despite the bright turquoise walls now completely free of the hideous wallpaper. Two gallons of lime green paint sat in the garage, waiting. Maybe she could persuade her father to help her start painting today. A big project like that would keep her busy until it was time to sleep again.

She rolled over and stretched, bumping her feet against a warm, solid object at the end of her bed.

"Sorry, Cleo," she said, "I didn't see you."

Unlike her human owner, Cleo never seemed to have a problem recapturing slumber. She stretched and yawned, then moved slowly up to Anna Mei's side and plopped down again. Anna Mei lay there for a long time, stroking the soft fur and shutting her eyes against the growing light.

Dragging herself out of bed an hour and a half later, she found her mother in the basement laundry room, feeding clothes into the washing machine.

"Good morning, sleepyhead," Mom said, reaching out to smooth Anna Mei's hair. "Is this a sneak peek of what it's going to be like having a teenager in the house?"

"I guess I was just tired," Anna Mei answered vaguely. "Where's Dad?"

"Off doing errands. He'll be back around lunchtime."

That put a kink in the whole bedroom painting idea. Now what was she going to do to fill up the day?

"Come and have some breakfast," Mom suggested, turning the knob to start the machine. "I could use a cup of coffee and some company."

They sat at the kitchen table, Anna Mei with her orange juice and bagel, her mother sipping from a mug that said *Nurses have lots of patience*. She remembered Mom explaining the pun to her when she was younger. It seemed like a long time ago, before things got so complicated.

"I can't believe it's almost Thanksgiving," her mother said now. "Look how bare the trees are already. And you can see geese migrating almost every day."

"Mmmmmm."

"Did I tell you we're invited to Aunt Karen's for Thanksgiving dinner?"

Anna Mei shrugged. "Maybe. I think so."

"I was thinking of trying out a new pie recipe," Mom said, not seeming to mind that she was pretty much carrying on the whole conversation by herself. "You put raisins and cranberries in with the apples."

The setting was so ordinary, her mother's voice so soothing and familiar, that Anna Mei was caught totally off guard when Mom reached out, stroked her cheek and said, "Please, honey, tell me what's wrong. Maybe I can help."

Something about that soft touch, so warm and tender against her face, seemed to melt Anna Mei's defenses. In a halting voice, full of stops and starts, she told her mother how much she had tried—*really* tried—to fit in here. But it just wasn't working.

"I never used to think about it before," she said. "Being Chinese, looking different from you and Dad and most everyone I know, never seemed important. But since we've been here, I've *had* to think about it. I can't get away from it."

Mom looked at her thoughtfully. "I wonder if it's really other people who are making you feel this way, or if moving here has just got you thinking about things in a new way. Has someone been teasing you about being adopted?"

"Well, no," Anna Mei said. "It's not like that. I just feel like I don't belong anywhere. All the other kids know where they came from, who their grandparents and great-grandparents were, sometimes centuries back. I'm not Danish like you, and I don't know anything about my Chinese ancestors."

"That's not exactly true," Mom said. "You know *one* thing—you know your mother wanted you to have a good life. That's why she brought you to the orphanage. She must have hoped that someday you'd have everything she couldn't give you herself."

Anna Mei felt her throat tighten and her eyes fill with tears, tears she'd never cried before for the stranger who was her birth mother. "Do you think . . . do you think she loved me?"

"I know she did," Mom answered without hesitation. "Remember the note I showed you, the one she pinned to your clothes? It said 'This is my daughter, Mei Li.' Your dad and I wanted to honor the name she gave you, but we added Anna, after *my* mother. That made you part of this family, too."

"Sometimes I wish I had more than Grandma's name. I wish I looked like I really belong in this family, like Emily and Benjamin."

"Anna Mei, there are so many kinds of belonging! And what do looks have to do with it? Think about it for a minute. Cleo doesn't look like you, either—doesn't she belong with you?"

"But that's different," Anna Mei protested.

"I don't see why. When it was time to choose a kitten you chose her—you said she was the exact kitten you were supposed to have. It's the same with us. There you were in China, and there we were in Massachusetts, but our hearts were a match. We were meant to be together. Your Dad and I just had to travel a long way to make it happen, that's all."

*"Daughter of my heart,"* Anna Mei said, repeating the phrase she'd grown up hearing. And for the first time, she thought she truly understood what it meant.

"Exactly," Mom said, putting her arms around Anna Mei and hugging her tight.

Anna Mei would have liked to stay like that all day. But something was still nagging at her.

"The thing is, I'm supposed to do this heritage report," she said. Then she told her mother about the assignment and how she'd been struggling to find a way to do it. "But I don't even know where to start," she said.

"Well, maybe it could be about your adoption instead of about your ancestors," Mom suggested. "You could explain that there are different ways to make a family."

"I don't know." Anna Mei felt doubtful. "That's not really what—"

They both looked up as the side door banged open and Anna Mei's father came in, his arms full of grocery bags.

"Here they are, my two best girls," he said. "And look who I found lurking in the driveway."

Danny was standing on the doorstep. "I just wanted to give back your lab coat," he said. "I keep forgetting to bring it to school."

"Good timing," her father told him. "I was just about to fix some lunch."

"Oh. Well . . . thanks, but I really can't stay. I have to . . . I mean, maybe some other time."

Moving quickly, before she could change her mind, Anna Mei scooted to the door and opened it wide. "Please, Danny," she said. "Please come in."

# Chapter Twenty

# TeamWork

Dad set the bags on the counter and started pulling out groceries. "Let's see . . . I bought stuff to make a pizza, or I could open a can of—"

"Dad?" Anna Mei broke in before he could recite the entire menu. "I kind of need to talk to Danny alone for a minute, okay?"

"But I—"

"Of course it's okay," her mother said, taking the milk out of his hand and putting it in the refrigerator. "I could use some help folding the laundry anyway. Come on, Greg."

He looked mystified but followed her down the basement stairs without further protest.

"I really can't stay," Danny said again. He stood just inside the door, still wearing his jacket and looking ready to make a run for it. "What do you want?"

"Just . . . to talk to you," she said.

"Yeah, I guess it's okay now, since no one else is around to see."

*Ouch.* He obviously wasn't going to make this easy on her. But she hadn't exactly been easy on him, either.

"That's what I wanted to talk about," she said. "I'm really sorry about the way I acted at the Follies, Danny. I was . . . I shouldn't have . . . it was a horrible thing to do. I hope you can forgive me."

He shrugged. "Why should you care?"

She hadn't prepared an answer to this question, but one came pretty easily: "Because I want us to be friends."

"Uh huh. And what will Zoey have to say about that?"

Anna Mei threw up her hands in exasperation. "Ugh! I am so *sick* of what Zoey has to say!"

"But . . ." He seemed confused at her change in tone. "I thought you liked her."

"I thought so, too, at first. I mean, I *wanted* to like her. I figured the faster I started making friends, the better. And Zoey asked me to join the Ponytails on the very first day I was here."

"Hey, *I* was nice on your first day!" he protested. "I thought you had the coolest name I ever heard."

"But I didn't know that at the time, remember? I thought you were making fun of it—making fun of *me*. I thought it was better to stick with Zoey and stay away from you. You can understand that, can't you?"

He seemed to let his guard down a little. "Yeah, I guess so. When you put it that way."

She grabbed her chance. "Come on, let's sit down," she said, gesturing toward the table. "I'll get us something to drink, okay?"

He came over and perched on a chair while she poured two glasses of milk. She noticed a package of cookies poking out of a grocery bag, so she grabbed that, too. After all, it was a tricky situation—a little sugar couldn't hurt.

"It's not like Zoey's a bad person," Anna Mei told him, "except for being kind of bossy, that is."

Danny snorted at the understatement, but she didn't give him a chance to interrupt. "Once I was in the club, though, I realized I didn't have much in common with those girls. I just pretended to be like them so they'd let me stay in it. Then pretty soon I was pretending a lot of things. I stopped saying what I really meant or telling people how I really felt, including my parents. And then you."

Danny took the cookie she offered and dunked it in his milk. "I still don't see why," he said.

She struggled to put her feelings into words. They were complicated—even she was just starting to figure them out. "I guess I thought if I had some friends, I would just blend in. People wouldn't think of me as the new girl, or the Chinese girl, or the adopted girl.

I could just be Anna Mei, like I was when we lived in Boston."

Danny swallowed the cookie and reached for another one. "Well, the way I see it, there's one tiny problem with that plan."

"And what exactly is that?" she wanted to know.

"I don't think anyone here has met Anna Mei yet. Except maybe me."

She frowned. What was he talking about? She'd lived here for three months now—of course people had met her. He wasn't making any sense.

"What do you—"

He didn't even let her finish the question. "I don't mean the one who shows up at school wearing a ponytail," he said. "I mean the real Anna Mei. The one who likes science but not horses. The one who likes bright pink shoes—whatever happened to those, anyway? The one who's smart and funny and has cool parents. If people ever get a chance to meet her, they won't care if she's from China or Saskatchewan or Mars."

It sounded so simple when he said it. How had she managed to make it so complicated?

"I don't know if that's true," she told him, "but I guess it's time to test the theory. Actually, I kind of wish I *was* from Mars. At least then I'd be able to do my heritage report: 'Greetings, earthlings, my name is Anna Mei and I come from a long line of scaly green Martians.'"

Danny, starting on his third cookie, paused in mid-dunk. "What's the problem with your heritage report?"

"I haven't been able to figure out what to say," she told him. "I'm named after my Danish grandmother, but I'm not really Danish, obviously. And I have the Chinese name my birth mother gave me, but I don't know who she was or where she came from. So which family do I choose?"

"Simple," he said, gulping down the last of his milk. "Neither."

"That's what I think, too. But I'll hate getting a zero for the assignment."

"No, I don't mean you shouldn't give a report, I mean you shouldn't choose. Anna and Mei are a team. You can't separate a team."

Anna Mei stared at him.

"What?" he asked. "Do I have crumbs stuck in my teeth or something?"

"Danny Gallagher, you're either brilliant . . . or completely crazy."

"Yeah, I get that a lot. Especially the crazy part." He grinned. "But what did I do?"

"You helped me figure out what my report should be about. It's going to be a little complicated, but I know my parents will help me. Assuming they ever come up from the basement, that is."

"Yeah, we may have to send a search and rescue team after them," he agreed.

She started to wrap up the cookies. "I'm glad you came over today, Danny. I really needed a friend, and then you showed up right on my doorstep. Thanks for giving me another chance."

"No sweat, Cartoon Girl," he said, with a grin that looked positively evil.

"I'm sorry it took so long, though. I know you had other things to do."

"Actually," he said, wiping his mouth with the napkin she handed him, "I was thinking I might hang around and try your dad's pizza."

# Chapter Twenty-One

# Goodbye, Ponytails

S itting down to eat that pizza was the last relaxing thing Anna Mei did the whole weekend. She spent the rest of the time working on her report—doing research, finding props, preparing special food. The hardest part was figuring out just the right words to say.

Once she had explained her idea to them, her parents jumped on board to help with the things she couldn't do alone. Her father didn't even complain about having to make another grocery store run.

By Monday morning Anna Mei had filled two large shopping bags with everything she needed for her presentation. Her mother was working a twelve-hour shift, so she was already at the hospital, but her father offered to drive her to school and help carry the extra bags.

Settling into the passenger seat of his car, Anna Mei noticed a bright pink envelope taped to the dashboard. On the front, in her mother's small, neat handwriting, were the words *Daughter of My Heart*.

She read the note as they drove the short distance to Elmwood Elementary.

> Dear Anna Mei,
>
> I'm sorry I can't be there this morning to wish you good luck in person. But I wanted you to know I'll be thinking of you, and that I'm very proud of all the hard work you did on this project. I've been working on a project myself! It's a secret for now but I hope to be able to tell you about it very soon.
>
> Always remember: "Jeg elsker dig." That's Danish for "I love you."
>
> Mom

Anna Mei tucked the note carefully into her backpack. Later today it would go in that special box where she kept her other treasures.

"She must have written it early this morning," Dad said.

"It was really nice of her," Anna Mei said. "In fact, you've both been really nice, considering the way I've been acting lately. I know I told you before, but I am sorry if it seemed like I was ashamed of you or Mom. Things just got a little crazy there for a while."

"So you're pleading temporary insanity, is that it?"

She laughed. "Something like that. It just took me a little while to figure things out."

"We knew that moving here would be an adjustment," he said. "We think you've handled it just fine. But I guess this means I shouldn't expect to see any more cowgirls in enormous boots, clomping around the house and scaring small animals?"

"No more cowgirls, Dad, I promise. I've had enough horsey stuff to last a lifetime. *Two* lifetimes."

She knew she needed to be a little more diplomatic with Zoey, Rachel, and Amber, though. At lunchtime, she broke the news that she had decided to resign from the Ponytail Club.

"I'm really glad you asked me to join," she said honestly. "I just don't think I'm going to have time right now."

"What do you mean?" Rachel asked.

"Well, Mr. Vogel has asked me to join the yearbook staff, for one thing. And Zandra wants me to try out for the volleyball team. I'm going to be pretty busy."

Zoey's eyes narrowed. "I hope you don't think you can drop out and then drop back in again, anytime you want."

Anna Mei was pretty certain that wouldn't be a

problem, but she tried to sound regretful about it. "Oh, sure, I understand," she said. "But I know you won't have any trouble filling my spot. It's such a great club."

Of course, that all depended on how you defined *great*, she supposed, but there was no point getting these girls mad at her. And they *had* been her very first friends here, even if it was only because they thought being from a big city made her special somehow. She owed them for that.

It wasn't until later in the afternoon that the butterflies came to attack her stomach. They kept at it right until the moment Ms. Wagner called her name, the moment she'd been dreading for weeks. Well, months, really. Danny offered an encouraging smile as she hauled her shopping bags to the front of the room.

*Okay, God,* Anna Mei found herself thinking, *you've gotten me this far figuring out your plan—you want me to be who I truly am. No more faking it for other people. Now if you could just throw in a couple ounces of courage to get me through the next few minutes, I'd be grateful.*

She turned to face the class, the same twenty-three pairs of eyes that had intimidated her so much on her very first day. But they seemed a lot more friendly now, or maybe she was just a lot less paranoid. Either way, she wasn't such a new kid anymore, and it was time to give her heritage report.

# Chapter Twenty-Two

# Introducing Anna Mei

"As you all know," she began, "my name is Anna Mei. Having a two-part name like that can be a pain sometimes, but I actually don't mind too much because there's a special reason for it. So my report is about these names, and how they both ended up being mine."

She reached into one of the bags and pulled out a long, silky dress. It had tiny cap sleeves and a high collar, and when she slipped it over her head, it fell in a straight, slim line down to the floor.

"I was born in China," she began, "in a province called Hunan. There are some big cities there, but also a lot of small towns and villages, where most of the people are farmers. In fact, Hunan is sometimes called 'the breadbasket of China.' And a lot of things we use in America—like rice, tea, and cotton—come from there."

As she talked, the words she'd practiced seemed to come more easily. "My family probably lived on a farm somewhere near a town called Yiyang. I know that because after I was born, my birth mother took me to the orphanage there. I think she probably couldn't take care of me herself, so she took me someplace where I'd be safe. But first she gave me a special name."

Anna Mei carefully removed a folded slip of paper from an envelope. She held it up so everyone could see the Chinese characters. "Here's the note she left on my clothes. It says: 'This is my daughter, Mei Li.' Mei Li is what she named me. It means 'Beautiful plum blossom.'"

She thought some of the kids might laugh at that part and was relieved when no one did. "I didn't live in Yiyang for very long, because pretty soon a couple named Gregory and Margaret Anderson came all the way from Massachusetts to adopt me."

She showed them the photo of her American parents, the one she kept on her dresser. "Here's a picture of us on the first day we met. It's pretty obvious why I don't remember it, though—I was only about eight months old."

Then she held up a piece of cloth embroidered with a picture of a mother panda bear and her cub. "Before we left China, we visited a city called Changsha, and my parents bought me this cloth. In China it means good luck. They also bought this Chinese dress I'm wearing, called a *qipao*. They wanted me to have some special things that came from the place where I was born."

Anna Mei let her eyes sweep the room. Everyone seemed to be interested—or at least, no one was yawning. She took a breath and kept going. "Now you know about Mei," she said, "so it's time to tell you a little about Anna."

She pulled more clothing out of her bag and started layering it right over the *qipao*. Soon she was wearing a white blouse and dark green vest. A bright blue sheet tied around her waist stood in for a skirt.

"Even though I was born in China, my adoptive family is Scandinavian," she said. "The Anna I'm named after was my grandmother on my mom's side. She told my mom a lot of stories about the old days in Denmark. Back then, the women wore outfits that looked something like this. Only there's one important thing missing."

She reached into the bag again and brought out a small white hat trimmed in lace, with ribbons that dangled from the front. "Young girls in Denmark always wore their hair in braids around their head. But as soon as they got married, they had to wear a cap, like this. It showed that they were already taken."

Anna Mei put the cap on and tied the ribbons under her chin. "This one belonged to my great-grandmother," she said, "the last of her family to be born in Denmark. She was proud of it because wearing a cap meant that she was a grown-up lady. She gave it to her daughter Anna, who gave it to my mother. And someday my mother will give it to me.

"My grandmother died last year, and I still really miss her. I wish she could tell me more stories about what things were like in the old days. But I'm glad I'll get to have something special that reminds me of her."

Her dry throat told her it was time to wrap this thing up. "All that's left in this bag are some treats my parents helped me make. These are spring rolls, one of many kinds of foods that are considered *dim sum*. That means 'touching your heart.' And these are Danish spice cookies, called . . . wait a minute, my mom wrote it down for me . . . called *krydderikager*. Luckily they taste better than they sound."

Now the kids laughed, but it was at her joke, not at her. The relief she felt at having gotten through her report made her feel a little light-headed. She started stuffing her costumes back into the bag while Ms. Wagner helped pass out the treats.

"I'm very impressed, Anna Mei," Ms. Wagner told her. "You obviously put a great deal of effort into this project."

"I know I actually gave two reports, Ms. Wagner, but it was the only way I could explain about my history. As someone truly brilliant once told me, Anna and Mei belong together."

In the back of the room, Danny was smiling. "Not bad, Cartoon Girl," he said, when she got back to her seat. "Not bad at all."

On the Wednesday night before Thanksgiving, Anna Mei lay sprawled across her bed, reading. Danny had loaned her a book about the history of anime, which she'd been surprised to discover was actually kind of interesting. Her mother was busy making raisin-cranberry-apple pies to take to Aunt Karen's for dinner, and her father had gone out on a mysterious errand, promising to explain later.

Cleo, sprawled out next to her, suddenly yawned and stretched. Then she padded over to stick her nose in Anna Mei's face, bumping and nudging her in the universal cat language that meant, "Put that thing down and feed me."

"All right, I get it," Anna Mei finally told her, rolling off the bed. "I was going to save you some turkey tomorrow, but now I'm not so sure."

Cleo ignored that remark and followed her to the kitchen, purring with gratitude when Anna Mei filled the empty bowl. The grinding whir of the garage door opener meant Dad was home—maybe now she'd find out what the big secret was. She met him coming in the side door.

"Hey, I wanted to surprise you!" he said, quickly hiding something behind his back.

"What is that?" she asked, trying to see around him. "It's not big enough to be that 50-inch flat screen TV you've been dreaming of."

"I'll probably still be dreaming of that when *I'm* fifty. But this stuff is for you—look."

He carried a shopping bag over to the table, then spilled out a jumble of scrapers, masking tape, paint brushes and rollers. "Since we have a three-day weekend coming up, I thought we'd finally get your bedroom painted."

Anna Mei reached over and hugged him. "Aw, thanks, Dad, that's really sweet. The only thing is . . . we're not quite ready to paint yet."

"What do you mean? The wallpaper is gone, and we already have the paint."

"Um, that's the thing." How could she put this gently? "That green paint? We're going to need to exchange it. For pink."

"But I thought—"

The oven timer went off, bringing Anna Mei's mother in to check on her pies. "What's all this?" she asked, looking at the mess on the table.

"Dad was surprising me with some painting stuff," Anna Mei said. "For my room."

"This must be the night for surprises, then," her mother said, "because I have one, too. I didn't want to tell you until I was sure, but I just got off the phone with Lauren's mother. She's letting Lauren come out for a visit during Christmas vacation."

Anna Mei whooped. Then shrieked. Then whooped again. She hugged her mother, then her father, then both of them. She danced around the kitchen until they chased her out, saying they felt exhausted just watching her.

Before collapsing into bed that night, Anna Mei dug through her backpack for the copy of the Irish blessing she'd gotten from Danny. She couldn't wait for Lauren to meet him—it would be the perfect blending of her old life with her new one.

She taped the scribbled note up on her still-turquoise-but-soon-to-be-pink wall so she could read it when she woke up tomorrow morning. It was a wish for all the things that truly mattered. All the things, she knew now, that she already had in abundance:

Walls for the wind,
A roof for the rain,
And tea beside the fire.
Laughter to cheer you,
Those you love near you,
And all that your heart may desire.

Anna Mei was almost asleep when she felt a warm, familiar weight plop onto the bed and snuggle up beside her. She reached out to stroke the silky fur around Cleo's ears, remembering a time when her cat had seemed like the only familiar and comforting thing in a strange new place.

"But we belong here now, don't we, Cleo?" Anna Mei whispered, pulling the blanket up over the two of them and closing her eyes again. In the dark, Cleo's soft, contented purr sounded like both an answer and a lullaby.

*Growing up*

in Michigan, Carol A. Grund spent a lot of time scribbling stories into notebooks. But it wasn't until she had three kids of her own that she knew she wanted to write for children. Her fiction and nonfiction have appeared in many magazines and several anthologies, including *Friend 2 Friend* and *Celebrate the Season!* (both from Pauline Books & Media) and *Ladybug, Ladybug* (Carus Publishing). *Anna Mei, Cartoon Girl* is her first novel. Watch for the next book in the Anna Mei series, coming in 2011! Read more about Carol and her work at www.CarolAGrund.com.

# The Stepping Stones Journals

### Written by Diana R. Jenkins

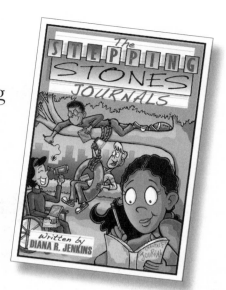

Alberto, Chantal, Denver, and Suki are back, but this time your friends from the popular *Stepping Stones* comics share their personal journals! In *The Stepping Stones Journals*, all four tell about the ups and downs of their lives in their own words—and you get to experience it firsthand. Like you, the *Stepping Stones* kids are dealing with family and friends, school and church, decisions and challenges. So follow along as they travel the stepping stones of life and journey toward a closer relationship to God!

Paperback
144 pp.
# 7129X
$8.95 U.S.

## Stepping Stones The Comic Collection

Paperback
128 pp.
# 71184
$9.95 U.S.

BOOKS & MEDIA

The Daughters of St. Paul operate book and media centers at the following addresses. Visit, call or write the one nearest you today, or find us on the World Wide Web, www.pauline.org

CALIFORNIA
3908 Sepulveda Blvd, Culver City, CA 90230          310-397-8676
2640 Broadway Street, Redwood City, CA 94063      650-369-4230
5945 Balboa Avenue, San Diego, CA 92111            858-565-9181

FLORIDA
145 S.W. 107th Avenue, Miami, FL 33174             305-559-6715

HAWAII
1143 Bishop Street, Honolulu, HI 96813             808-521-2731
Neighbor Islands call:          866-521-2731

ILLINOIS
172 North Michigan Avenue, Chicago, IL 60601       312-346-4228

LOUISIANA
4403 Veterans Memorial Blvd, Metairie, LA 70006    504-887-7631

MASSACHUSETTS
885 Providence Hwy, Dedham, MA 02026               781-326-5385

MISSOURI
9804 Watson Road, St. Louis, MO 63126              314-965-3512

NEW YORK
64 West 38th Street, New York, NY 10018            212-754-1110

PENNSYLVANIA
9171-A Roosevelt Blvd, Philadelphia, PA 19114      215-676-9494

SOUTH CAROLINA
243 King Street, Charleston, SC 29401              843-577-0175

VIRGINIA
1025 King Street, Alexandria, VA 22314             703-549-3806

CANADA
3022 Dufferin Street, Toronto, ON M6B 3T5          416-781-9131